Dedicated to my good friends Umit and Dave.
A big thanks to my family – it's been too long and!
And to the Eurogamer novel writing crew – thanks for all your support and guidance.

Most of all a big thanks to my readers, I hope you continue to enjoy my work for many years to come.

Keep up with my latest news and releases via my blog:

http://thecultofme.blogspot.co.uk/

You can also follow me on Twitter:

http://www.twitter.com/TheCultofMe

This second edition of The Cult of Me was edited by Alex Roddie from Pinnacle Editorial:

http://www.pinnacleeditorial.co.uk/

© 2011 – 2012 Michael Brookes All rights reserved

Chapter 1
The first night

The shout for lights out echoed along the corridor, accompanied by the jingle of keys that signified a prison guard on patrol. The lights in all of our cells snapped off, leaving me alone in the darkness. This was my first night in Her Majesty's Prison. For most this would be a fearful event, but for me only the first step in the plan for my last stand.

The darkness wasn't total. A shaft of pallid light from the security lamps outside leaked through the tiny window. The bars set into the concrete sliced shadows into the weak glow. I saw the toilet, shrouded in gloom in the far corner, the slatted privacy barrier collapsed against the sink next to it. In the opposite corner stood a simple wooden table and matching chair, now only visible as shaded forms beneath the window.

I lay still upon the bed and absorbed the atmosphere around me. With my heightened senses I smelt the fear and rage from the occupants of the cells nearby. It was a satisfying scent that reminded me that here was exactly where I needed to be. Beneath me, the thin mattress failed to prevent the metal slats digging into the bruises that covered my back: fully deserved bruises I should add. You don't kill several people in broad daylight, including two police officers, without some repercussions.

Despite the pain, or maybe even because of it, I felt content — more content than I had been in a very long time. It felt good to rest after such a busy day. I guessed in some way I should be thankful that all I received were a few bruises from those well placed blows... Petty revenge really considering the deeds I committed. The first stage of my plan was now complete. There would be a reckoning, but not yet, for now I was content to lie still and drift through my new surroundings.

Every half hour the flap in the cell door slapped open, and stern eyes peered through to make sure I still lived. They took such care of all new prisoners, especially those who were never likely to see the outside world again. On that first day only two new prisoners were admitted: me and the man now sobbing at the far end of the corridor. They didn't need to be concerned about me. I was exactly where I wanted to be. Him on the other hand — well, we'll get to him shortly.

At ease in the darkness and listened to the unfamiliar sounds. At the far end of the cell water gurgled through a large pipe in its vain attempt to warm the chill air. The thin prison issue blankets provided little warmth, but that didn't matter. It was still warmer here than on the streets where I lived for the past few years. Besides, I now had a purpose, and that brought its own warmth.

From all around the prison I heard noises, mostly voices. I listened to snatches of conversation. All used the peculiar patois common to those that have been incarcerated. It was like learning a new language. Ordinarily it would have taken time for a newcomer like me to learn the intricacies of this language, but I had an advantage. I just plucked the knowledge from the minds of the experienced cons.

Beneath the chatter I detected an undercurrent of fear. I sensed from their thoughts that even for the old hands this could be a frightening place. Violence often erupted easily, whether from the guards or from the other prisoners. I didn't mind: for me it took more than tall concrete walls to cage my will.

I smiled as I remembered the short poem a previous occupant had scrawled on the wall:

> "If these walls were made of blow,
> I'd smoke a hole and away I'd go.
> But as they're made of brick and stone,
> I leave the fucking things alone."

The same wit, obviously in fine form, had labelled the emergency bell. Above it he'd written "Push button for sex!" and below the red button "When pressed a cunt will appear." It pleased me to know that, even in this place, some humour remained. The guard who escorted me to this cell warned me against pressing the button: "I had better be dying or I soon would be," had been his eloquent warning. He needn't have worried. I wouldn't be dying here, not yet at any rate.

In the cell beside me, I heard the soft rhythmic sound of a man masturbating himself to sleep. I relaxed and expanded my awareness, allowed it to drift through the wall and into his cell. Being able to leave the confines of my mind had been a talent of mine for many years.

Well, well. That wasn't something you saw every day. In his mind he pictured a pretty blonde, much older than himself. Her body was well formed and all too familiar to this man. She certainly appeared to be enjoying his energetic exertions. Delving deeper I discovered that this was no ordinary blonde fantasy; the women in question was much closer to him. I smiled to myself. His mother possessed a fine figure, well worth the attentions of an obedient son. Not that my tastes ran that way, you understand.

As always he detected my intrusion and it disrupted his rhythm. It always annoyed me that people detected my presence. Luckily for me, most people paid little attention to their mind's warnings and ignored me. Anyway, disturbing a man mid-stroke seemed a little impolite, so I withdrew and left him to his solitary pleasures.

I mentally shrugged and let my awareness drift down the corridor, past the patrolling guard. With my mind's eye I saw him clearly; his sharply pressed black trousers, polished shoes, crisp white shirt and black tie. He walked carefully and deliberately along the corridor. His mind followed the familiar routine, but he still relied on his instincts for any change in atmosphere.

Along each side lay a bank of eight cells, all maximum security as befitting category A prisoners. Every convict on this wing had been deemed a serious risk to the public. Even so everyone in this wing had demonstrated a taste for murder or rape, the kind of acts that excited the newspapers so much. Every prisoner had their own bloody tale to tell.

Normally a remand prisoner wouldn't be included in such exalted company, but as the court deemed me a significant threat to public safety the court ordered me in with the convicted felons. I was forced to wear the special striped denim uniform and not my usual street clothes. That wasn't a great hardship. My street clothes acquired many unusual smells over the years.

Being housed in the security wing brought mixed blessings. On the positive side it provided access to the more dangerous prisoners - they would prove essential for my plan. On the other hand it meant that my movements would be restricted and that I'd be kept under closer observation.

The guard stopped by the door for a few seconds, long enough to open the flap and check that I still lived. From his eyes I saw my own vague form, as if asleep on the bed.

At the far end of the corridor whimpered the other prisoner from the day's intake. His sobs marked him out as fresh prey and already he found himself surrounded by the catcalls of the prisoners in the neighbouring cells.

I slipped into his mind easily, like a worm through soil. I encountered no resistance, only horrified confusion. The chaos inside him appeared driven by two great conflicts. The first was the emerging realisation of his guilt and the act that caused it; the second was his rapidly growing need for a fix. Satisfying the second would drive away the first, if only for a little while. Sadly for him, no such escape could be found here, not on the first night — and most definitely not without the right friends.

A quick fix would take the pain away - and not just the pain of withdrawal, but also the pain of the memory of the deed he committed. Even now he barely remembered, but I could see with great clarity the dreadful crime he perpetrated, the sin which even the murderers and rapists around him would never forgive him for. Like me they already knew the truth. The grapevine informed everyone before he even arrived, and with eager anticipation they waited for him.

The prison guards were right to maintain a watch on this one. If he had the means and the will then I doubted that he would last the night. The fever that gripped him caused enough pain on its own to make him seek that final option. He barely remembered what he had done, the terrible crime that he committed. I could help him remember, lay every detail out for him to relive. It pleased me to do so.

His cries increased in volume, shrill with grief. His mind fractured under this new torment as I revealed the truth to him. First I resurrected the vision of his young daughter, only weeks from the womb. She looked tiny, wrinkled and vulnerable. My second action created the sounds of her crying, seeking attention and nourishment. That provided the trigger for his own memories.

For him, it seemed a lifetime since he waited alone in the squalid flat. The mother was not there. She'd left some hours previously to score the drug they needed: the brown powder that would bring the relief he craved. For now he sat alone with the child, bombarded by her shrieks for attention. All he wanted was for her to be silent. Not too much to ask, he thought; all too quickly his temper snapped and he grabbed her from the cot.

With a shout and a shake she fell silent.

Unaware of what he had done, he dropped her back in the cot, now satisfied with the peace and quiet. Neither he nor the mother noticed the silent corpse slowly turning blue as they got high. She went unnoticed until the visit from the social worker the next day, and then he knew only the frenzied confusion that ended with him here, alone in his cell, surrounded by the baying wolves.

Unfortunately for him, he wasn't alone. I would help him remember. Like a proxy conscience I resurrected his dead daughter and smiled as his screams echoed from the walls that closed in on him. His screams just goaded the killers around him. They shouted through the gaps in their doors and through the windows, promising him torments even greater than the one he currently experienced.

He looked at those same hands now. They looked the same as they did before. It seemed strange to him that he could see them with such clarity. He barely heard the rough voices around him, the promises of what would happen to him in the days to come. I withdrew and left him to his misery. There was no real sport there. With a nudge it would be easy to convince him of what must be done, but why waste the effort? His fate was already sealed, and I had more fun times ahead of me. If by some miracle he survived the next day then I could visit him again.

With no effort at all I returned to my body, lying on the hard bed. I felt contented and allowed myself to sleep and to dream.

Chapter 2
My first kill

Prison provided plenty of time for introspection for inmates, and I proved no exception. Locked up for twenty three hours a day, the minds of the prisoners around me soon became stale — so I succumbed, letting my thoughts wander down the path that led me to this place.

I didn't follow the pattern of most mass murderers. I didn't wet my bed, I was never abused as a child and for the most part my childhood was a happy one. There were a few events that helped me discover my unique ability. Soon after my twelfth birthday I experienced the first hint that I might be different to other people.

For all the years I could remember I grew up in Lewes: a quaint, historical town back then, nestled in the bosom of the South Downs. We moved there after my father died. I was four years old at the time.

My father died before I was old enough to know him, so my memories of him came from old photographs and from my mother's own recollections. He was a good man I had never known. My mother worked as a mid-level clerk at a local bank, which meant I spent more time alone than most kids my age.

That's not to say I didn't have friends. I did, but for the most part I preferred my own company. If the weather turned bad then I spent my time reading: mostly young adventure books, but also some serious stuff about astronomy and whatever attracted my interest. At the time I seemed to become interested in new things on a daily basis.

The stars always fascinated me. Even now I think there is nothing more beautiful than a crisp, clear night sky. I've always experienced a wonder when contemplating it, a mystery that caught my attention. In fact, at that age, I dreamed that I would become an astronomer, and dedicate my life to unlocking its mysteries. Alas, that pleasant little fiction was not to be.

When the weather was nice I ventured out. I loved to explore, and the town and the surrounding countryside provided plenty of opportunity. The old castle dominated the centre of the town: one of the first built by the Normans after their invasion in 1066. I loved climbing to the top of the battered keep to look out across the hills. The view from the battlements was spectacular. You could see for miles in every direction.

The Downs themselves surrounded the town: rolling chalk hills, lush with grass. Either on foot or by bike I journeyed out into the hills to discover new places. As long as I returned home by early evening and didn't get into any trouble, my mother didn't mind how I spent my time.

One exception occurred the previous summer. I dug my own cave in the nearby chalk pits. She wasn't amused by me returning home every evening covered in chalk dust. Luckily she didn't notice the missing pick-axe and shovel from the garden shed.

Many famous landmarks around the area were firm favourites. The Long Man was one of them: a giant chalk outline of a primitive man, cut into the side of a hill, visible from many miles away. Amusingly he dangled a twenty foot penis.

I remembered a persistent rumour that the police sealed the area off every Halloween. Apparently people who wandered in would disappear. The kids whispered that a satanic cult practised their black arts and the missing were the victims of their rituals. The occasional news on the television of children being rescued by Social Services from cults only served to add credence to these rumours.

As well as the famous places, I also enjoyed more secret haunts. These were secluded and special to me. A short trek through the woods along a mirror bright stream brought me to the chalk pits. It was here I dug my cave and it was here that I would later kill my first living being. We'll get to that soon.

The summit of the chalk pits consisted of a series of depressions and little gullies. Kids of all ages took their bikes up there and raced around. The local council eventually fenced the area off when Gavin Stoakes, an eight year old boy from my school, missed one of the jumps and fell into the pits below.

Luckily for him he only broke his arm and both legs, but the accident triggered a noisy campaign from some of the parents. The council eventually listened and so we were all banned from going there anymore.

The river Ouse meandered on the other side of town: a slow, wide river with Second World War pillboxes dotted along its length. These small brick and concrete fortifications were fascinating places for me. Slits for the machineguns covered the approaches of the river. Unfortunately the machine guns were no longer there, but they still made great places to play in. They smelled musty inside and you could imagine the soldiers in these cramped fortifications, scanning the river for German invaders.

Local farmers grazed their cattle along the river and the animals watched with bovine indifference whenever we played. In one popular game a group attacked the pillbox while the others defended it. Generally the weapons of choice were catapults or elastic bands with paperclips. I developed a new weapon — the shit grenade. You picked up a cow pat with a stick and tried to throw it through the weapon slits. As with most biological weapons, it was swiftly banned by the authorities (our parents).

Patches of fields and copses of dark trees covered the Downs. Each year as I grew, I explored further out than in previous holidays. Sometimes I pressed my luck by going too far, and I would have to race the sun to get home before my tea was put on the table.

On these runs I discovered that I was faster and stronger than I realised. I could run several miles without stopping for breath. Soon after starting secondary school I was invited to join the cross country running team, and I often beat older boys in the gruelling long distance races in all weathers. I have to confess, it did feel good to win.

The Downs presented contradictions, which was part of the joy of the place. Near the old hill fort, prison walls loomed over the surrounding grassland: a curse on the beautiful landscape. The prison became a source of much speculation. As a child I had no real experience of crime or criminals, so I wondered who it was they put in this forbidding place. I need speculate no longer.

Just a few miles from the prison I found a large open area used to train horses. Occasionally I would sit and watch them sprint back and forth. Unlike most of the

Downs, the grass here was always cropped short, more like a garden lawn than a meadow. Fragments of ancient forest broke up the patchwork of fields. There I hid from everyone in amongst the shadows of the trees. Springs gushed from the chalk, cool no matter how hot the sun shone.

Once, inside a copse enclosed by a broken fence, I discovered a tiny graveyard. The gravestones were so worn I couldn't read the inscriptions. One of the plots, covered by a stone slab, appeared to be more of a tomb than a grave. I tried to move the stone to see inside, thrilled with the expectation of seeing a skeleton, but sadly the slab was too heavy for even me to move.

It was a place of wonder for a growing boy who loved to explore and, even now, I sometimes find myself wishing I could return to that time. Of all the marvels I found, the place I always returned to was the chalk pits. My mother didn't like me going there — not just because of covering myself in chalk dust, but because to get to it, you had to cross a busy road. She worried about that, as all mothers do. But I found a secret way, a way under the road through an old dried-out culvert that meant I could cross without having to worry about the speeding traffic.

To get there from where I lived I wandered to the end of my street and followed the road to the old rubbish dump. The dump itself was another place of fascination and here one could find all sorts of abandoned treasures. Of course that was somewhere else that my mother didn't like me to go, and neither did the old man who managed the place. Thankfully he wasn't always there, so it was sometimes possible to sneak in and rummage through what had been discarded. The tip also provided a handy shortcut to the woods beyond.

A clear stream cut through the woods. If you sat and watched, you could see all kinds of small fish darting about. Beyond the stream were the railway tracks and, past them, the river itself. Following the path through the woods, about a mile in, you turned left from the path and then climbed a bank so steep I'd have to use the trees to help me clamber up the slope. From here you edged along until you reached the culvert and through this and under the road to the entrance of the chalk pits.

Just inside the chalk pits there stood an old pub, long abandoned and boarded up. Once I broke in to have a look round, but found nothing of interest, just some wrecked and mouldy furniture. The floor of the chalk pits was overgrown with bushes and small trees. Out of sight at the back was the small cave I had patiently dug the year before. As I approached this historic monument of mine I heard a strange noise — sad, like a whimper or a moan.

Quietly, I tracked the sound until I found its source under a small bush. Here I discovered a young fox: not a cub, but not a full grown adult either. The back end of this animal had been crushed, most likely from being hit by a car on the road. It must have dragged itself all this way before running out of strength. As I approached, the animal bared its teeth at me and tried to escape, but its efforts were pitiful and it could move no further.

Looking at this poor creature, I felt a pang of sadness — and also a stranger sensation. It was as if the pain the fox was feeling was also inside my own head. This thought startled me, but once imagined I couldn't shake this pain from inside me.

I retreated, desperate to escape this feeling. I did not want to share this creature's torment, but moving away did not weaken the sensation. Even when I reached the road the pain didn't diminish. I approached the animal once again. It didn't even raise its head this time. Beside it lay a small flint rock, twice as large as its head. I knew that I could end its suffering and, with it, this uncomfortable sensation in my mind.

I lifted the rock. The fox tracked it with its eyes. I lifted the weapon high and with a swift movement smashed it into the fox's skull. With that first blow it whimpered once, and with the second it was silent.

I smiled.

Chapter 3
My first wake up

The lights for the hallway and the cells all switched on together, accompanied by the march of boots and the rattle of keys. Despite the uncomfortable bed and thin blankets that did little to stave off the cold I'd slept well. It was, after all, a step up from the harder and colder streets where I had slept only a day before.

After the simple satisfaction of relieving myself I stood before the sink and splashed cold water onto my face. The water's chill pushed away sleep's fugue. I examined myself in the polished metal tile they provided us with to use as a mirror. A large bruise discoloured one side of my face, and a day's growth shadowed my cheeks and neck.

This would be my first public appearance, so I tried to make some effort. I washed myself with cheap soap and then wished I'd been allowed a razor. It would have to do.

A few minutes later I finished, refreshed and ready for the day ahead. The guards marched up and down the corridor, shouting and checking that everyone was awake. Lazing in bed was not an option — and to refuse orders was a punishable offence.

Shouted instructions from the guards indicated that breakfast would be served in ten minutes. We must all be ready to leave our cells before then. I dressed in the prison issue uniform, blue and white striped shirt, loose jeans and stiff black boots. As a category A prisoner I also wore the stylish yellow stripe down the left side.

I then made my bed in the regulation manner. It's the first thing they taught me: the cell must be kept clean and the bed always made properly unless it was night time and I was sleeping in it. These little rules that reinforced the big one. Do as you are told I didn't mind. Let them enjoy their petty victories while they could. Thinking back, maybe I should have made more of the opportunities I had then. Still, such insights are always easy with the benefit of hindsight.

A commotion from the end of the hall attracted my attention. Somebody wasn't obeying orders as quickly as they should. It was no surprise when I heard the other new intake's whining at the centre of the trouble. Just as much as the screws, convicts hated any change in routine and I heard grumbling and the odd shout for him to get his fucking arse in gear.

I took a moment to ponder my situation. Now, in the metaphorical cold light of day, I experienced some doubts. I could so easily be still outside these walls. For years I acted unseen from the shadows, delivering my own personal flavoured doom into people's lives.

For twenty odd years I operated without detection or even suspicion, or at least without anyone suspecting for very long. And now I was going public, not just here in the prison, but in the imminent court case as well. None of these poor fools realised what was coming.

But at the heart of the matter was that I went there to die. It seems an odd thing now, but back then I was tired. I no longer experienced the same satisfaction that I once did. So there I was, ready for that last stand. They might not have been ready for me, but human beings have always been adaptable creatures. Once I unleashed hell upon them, they would find a way to stop me — or at least I hoped they would. I wanted to end on a high note.

But not yet, there would be no endings on that day. That day was marked as a day of beginnings. First I would take little steps. I needed to sow the seeds that would eventually grow into my ownership of this prison … not just the hearts and minds, but the body and soul of every living person in there. To move too quickly would spoil the entertainments I planned for the coming court case. Once judged I could move onto the next stage.

For that first day I only needed to accomplish a small thing: I had to earn that first kernel of respect. I already had some of that with the other prisoners. A murderer, especially one who has just killed five people — including two police officers with his bare hands in a busy city street — would automatically be treated with caution.

Word had already spread. No doubt I was featured in the morning news, but as with everything, people needed to see things with their own eyes. I would need an eager volunteer to use as an example. I felt sure that somebody wouldn't disappoint me.

Even superficial observation revealed that there were two tribes in here, both as violent and, in their own way, as dangerous as the other. I assumed the convicts would be relatively easy to deal with. Some judicious violence would do the trick.

I needed to be more circumspect with the officers. They presented a law unto themselves and were used to bending it in their daily battle to maintain order. They wouldn't be as impressed by a show of strength and they certainly wouldn't feel any respect for a cop-killer.

The cell doors opened one by one, disturbing my musing. The guards let us out one group at a time to collect our breakfast before returning us to our cells. It felt good to stretch the legs a little, everything a little stiff. Along with my other talents I had always healed quickly, so I felt better than I did the day before.

I walked out into the corridor where everything looked bright: pale walls and shiny floor, both kept meticulously clean by the prisoners now leaving their cells.

I took the opportunity to see my fellow travellers in the flesh. Apart from one or two exceptions they could all have been cast from the same mould. Sure, they all looked different — some big and bulky, others small and wiry, and all variations, colours and ages in between — but they all had the same eyes. In war films they called it the "Thousand yard stare". They are the eyes of people who had seen things that others have not — the eyes of those who lived in a constant world of danger and, while most of them wouldn't admit it, fear.

A few of the bolder ones stared back, sized me up. Some nodded, graciously acknowledging my existence. Maybe they thought they knew who I was.

Our sobbing friend from the night before made his grand entrance: a rabbit surrounded by wolves. Everyone read the panic in his furtive movements. He knew that a dozen predators now watched him hungrily. He tried to keep close to the guards, like a baby fawn in the herd. It was clear to everyone that for his crimes, the only protection he could hope for was solitary confinement.

Once there, for a lifer like him, confinement meant a slow descent into misery and lonely death. He wouldn't know that, of course. The lure of safety would override other concerns.

Two guards strode between the prisoners. They were lions amongst the wolves. Despite being outnumbered they showed only strength, emboldened by the uniforms and what they represented. They might be outnumbered, but they were a force that worked together. Even the gangs couldn't match their organisation.

The guards corralled us towards the stairs, through the first set of steel gates. Another officer waited, watching us all closely as we passed by.

We walked down the stairs towards the mess hall. In other wings we would be permitted to eat together, but it would have been dangerous to allow this here. As we arrived near the counter where the breakfast was laid out, I found the smell surprisingly enticing. With some annoyance I experienced an itch at the back of my neck.

It seemed my little demonstration would happen a bit sooner than I expected. No matter: now, the next day, or any other day would do. It had to happen sometime ... although, as my salivating mouth pointed out, it would have been nice to have eaten first.

The breakfast was laid out on large metal trays, stringy bacon in one, small sausages in another, both swimming in brown grease. Other trays provided a choice of fried or scrambled eggs. Some toast, some porridge. All in all not a bad meal: it really was a shame I would miss it.

The waiting line shuffled onwards, nearer to the food. I picked up a tray and a plastic mug for tea or coffee. After another step I sensed movement from behind. The moment approached.

I cast my mind out and I saw Peterson, a giant beast of a man, as he pushed his way through the line towards me. I delved into his mind and learned that he was serving life for an armed robbery that went wrong and ended with a dead cashier. A violent man who was too used to easy victories, even in here, Peterson had no idea of the mistake he was about to make.

In one hand he gripped a sock with a large battery inside it: a common and surprisingly effective weapon in prison. I delved a little deeper and saw that he had been paid to do this. Two hundred real cigarettes, rather than cheap rollups, waited for him back in his cell. Sure enough, the guards dotted around the hall all studiously ignored his movement. Only the officer positioned behind the food counter didn't seem to be in on it, but he hadn't noticed anything yet.

The other prisoners moved out of his way. A loner that not even those with connections messed with, Peterson possessed an evil reputation. I held my nerve and let him approach.

He swung the sock. As I ducked and span towards him, the weighted sock swept over my head. I rose from the crouch and jabbed the metal tray straight into his throat. He collapsed to the ground, frantically gasping for air.

The guards reacted, blowing their whistles as they summoned back-up. Some of them moved the prisoners against the wall, where they had to wait on their knees for the excitement to finish. The prisoners shouted words of encouragement. Everyone likes to see a big man fall. A few judicious jabs from truncheons silenced their enthusiasm.

Before the nearest of the two guards reached me I dropped the tray and lay on the ground face first. I already knew the drill and offered no resistance. One of them managed a sly kick to the ribs before securing my wrists with plastic cable ties and lifted me from the floor.

They escorted me to the block. It was only a short walk but I enjoyed the open air while it lasted. The sun shone brightly: a lovely winter's day, the air felt brisk, but the sun warmed my face. My ribs hurt a little, but already the pain started to fade. Within minutes I'm pushed into a new cell, this one much sparser than the other. The block was where they took prisoners for special punishment and in here even defending oneself was a crime.

What did annoy me, though, is that I felt hungry and I wouldn't be fed until lunchtime. That hardly seemed fair to me.

Chapter 4
A few days in the block

After cutting the bonds to free my hands and scrawling my name and number on the door the guards left me to wait. I took the time to investigate my new surroundings. This cell was very different from the one back at the wing. The door looked cunningly designed so that it could open both ways, so there was no way I could barricade myself in. Not that there was anything with which to build a barricade.

The door also had an odd circular hole in it. After a moment I realised that it was for a fire hose. If I started a fire they could put it out without having to open the door. Very clever! It also occurred to me that it would be a handy way to pacify an angry prisoner. One thing remained the same. The cell had the same narrow slit, with a flap on the other side, through which they could have a peek whenever they wanted.

I paced for a time and measured the cell. It was smaller, although the ceiling was higher and the single mesh covered light was out of reach. Set into the outside wall was a narrow window that couldn't be opened. I saw only fence and sky through it. This was a prison within a prison.

The cell contained no bed, just a wooden board set into the concrete floor and, most fascinating of all, two pieces of furniture: a small table and a chair. I inspected them closely. They were made from corrugated cardboard that had been folded several times for extra strength. Gingerly I tested the chair and it carried my weight without protest. As an experiment I jumped on the chair and it still stood strong.

Yes, that really was how bored I felt.

Thankfully, some time after noon they brought me some lunch. The tray passed through the slit in the door. The meal consisted of bland boiled food accompanied by a cup of unsweetened tea. A feast fit for a king! Well, it was edible at any rate and did help calm the pangs that rose in volume throughout the morning. A good thing too, it had been some time since I last ate.

After lunch two different officers escorted me from the cell, led me down the brightly lit corridor and into what can only be described as a little courtroom. The two guards stood beside me and I had to stand as more officers and one of the prison governors strode into the room. I paid the officers no heed, but the governor interested me.

I dipped into his mind. I sensed his discomfort as I rummaged through his thoughts and memories, but happily ignored it. Here was a man used to dealing with violent offenders, having been previously posted at the infamous Maze Prison in Northern Ireland. There he ran a jail full of terrorists and sectarian thugs. It must have been a step down to be here, and I wondered why. I delved deeper and soon found the answer. Now this was interesting — his name was down on an active target list.

Other memories provided me with information about his family. I saw his wife of thirty years and three children, all in their teens. I wondered how much he really cared for that pretty family of his. That could provide useful leverage, but that was a question for another day. Today I would just toe the line — or that was certainly my intention. Sometimes my temper got the better of me.

I stood to attention as the senior officer read the charge out. It boiled down to fighting and refusing to obey a lawful order. There listed a number of witnesses, mostly guards. Only one prisoner, my sobbing friend from the night before, was willing to speak as a witness.

This was the price he had to pay for a life in solitary confinement for his own protection. Oh Jonathan, I thought to myself, a moment ago you were just a nonce. A target, nothing special, but now you've made yourself a grass and even the nonces will hate you.

That made little difference to me. My guilt was clear. After a speech about keeping my nose clean and other pointless platitudes the stern faced governor asked if I had anything to say on my own behalf.

"I do. First, since when has it been a crime to defend oneself? I notice your little troopers missed out the fact that I was attacked. I started no trouble and was merely waiting for my breakfast."

"The rules are clear," he declared. "Fighting is not permitted, under any circumstances."

I was incredulous. "So I should have just stood there and waited for these officers to have actually noticed what was going on?" I shook my head. "Surely I have the right to defend myself."

"My officers are responsible for the safety of all prisoners." With this he leaned forward. "In here you have only the rights we give you. You would do well to remember this. Now, unless you have anything pertinent to add?"

I should have kept silent. Now wasn't the time to start messing with the guards — it was too soon, but his smug, imperious tone annoyed me.

"Actually, there is just one thing. What of the fact that the attack was instigated by one of your own officers?"

He smiled, knowing that there was no way I could prove this and demanded as such. I matched his smile and turned to one of the officers beside me. I had never seen this man before and he certainly hadn't been anywhere near the altercation. With a startled expression on his face we all heard him say "It's true sir. I paid Peterson two hundred cigarettes to attack this prisoner sir." He snapped his mouth shut, suddenly mortified by what he just said.

My smile broadened as the Governor's slipped. He glared at the confessing officer.

"I will of course have to investigate this matter, but no matter what the cause, fighting is still against the rules. In light of these mitigating circumstances I will restrict the punishment to four days cellular confinement. Now take him back to his cell."

If the officers were a little rough taking me back to the cell, I couldn't really blame them. None of them really understood what had just happened. I could, of course, have taken it further, but now was not the time. I shouldn't have allowed that little moment of pique to get the better of me. No matter. I would do my four days quietly, catch up on some rest and be back on the wing by Sunday.

The rest of the day passed quietly. When the evening meal was served somebody whispered through the door "I don't know what you did, but it was nicely done!" It's nice to be appreciated I thought as I slowly ate the curry with too many peas in it.

Just before eight pm the cell door opened and a thin mattress and a couple of blankets were thrown in. Some comfort at last.

After breakfast the next day the guards disturbed me again, this time for a trip to court for a bail appearance. We all knew this was a waste of time and, besides, I'd already declined legal representation. I refused to go. This caused some consternation at first and some calls back and forth, but in the end they left me in peace.

I quickly grew bored and asked for some reading material. I wasn't expecting much, but apparently even that was too much to ask. It seemed that cellular confinement meant a complete loss of privileges.

No privileges meant I'd receive no items from my canteen — not that I had been given chance to go to canteen yet — no books, and no smokes. Luckily, as with any good rule I plucked a loophole from the surface of one of the guard's mind. By law you are always allowed access to your religious text, so I became Christian for a few days and they let me have a Bible.

It was a pretty good read. Don't get me wrong, it had some boring bits, but there were some juicy bits too. Don't worry. I won't spoil the ending for you.

On the third day a commotion in the cell next door destroyed the tranquillity. It was clearly an angry young man who felt he was being unjustly treated. For far too long he kicked and punched his door. I can assure you that kicking a steel door makes a lot of noise in a confined space. He shouted curses at anyone and everyone. I tried to continue reading, expecting him to tire. I clearly underestimated his stamina.

We're not supposed to talk to other prisoners while confined in the block, but everyone broke the rule in this instance. Both guards and prisoners told him to shut up, but he wouldn't listen.

As I wasn't getting any more reading done for a while I went for a little dip inside his head. His thoughts identified him as a gangster wannabe who robbed drug dealers for a living. Apparently he'd been a bit clumsy with his firearms and shot one of the girls in the house of the last dealer he had robbed. So now he was not only serving life, with a minimum of ten years, but he also had one of the most connected dealers in the city chasing him.

The irony here was that he'd actually been moved straight from reception into the block for his own safety. If only he kept his mouth shut that might have been true.

I took a firm grip of his mind and dragged it forward. His body immediately followed. His face smashed into the door, and I saw a bright light burst inside his head as it connected. I pulled his head back, and smashed it forward again. Unfortunately for him he started to beg for something or other as I did this. His mouth opened as it hit the door. Again the burst of light, this time tinged with red. I decided on a third time for good measure and I swear I didn't know this was going to happen. A guard opened the door at the same as I drove his head forward. The two met with a crunch. There was no burst of light this time, just a darkness that sucked his mind from my grasp.

The officers assumed that the wounds were self inflicted and transferred him to the hospital wing. Luckily the sound of another prisoner mopping up the blood didn't disturb my reading at all.

Chapter 5
My first proper kill

Almost a year passed since I killed that young fox. I didn't kill anything else in that time. I didn't suddenly develop a taste for torturing small animals or small humans for that matter. Life continued on as it had before. Despite being early September the weather was still glorious. I'd enjoyed another wonderful summer holiday exploring my favourite haunts and discovering new secrets. Now school claimed my time.

That year I started my second year at secondary school, a small church-run comprehensive. My mother and I weren't regular church goers, but it was apparently one of the best schools in the area so she pulled a few strings to get me in. I guess being well known in the local bank had its advantages. As I was about to discover, it had its downside too.

I can't remember exactly what time it was when I woke, but something disturbed my slumber. For a short time I lay there, staring up at the silhouettes of my model planes hanging on threads from the ceiling in mock battle. I guessed the hour must have been quite late as the glow in the dark stars that dotted the ceiling had lost their feeble shine.

My senses have always been better than most people's. I can hear things they can't and smell things before they do.

My eyesight always tested perfectly. A muffled noise from my mother's bedroom grabbed my attention. I rarely heard any noise from her room at night, so I strained to hear. As I listened I caught another unidentified sound followed by some footsteps — footsteps that sounded heavier than my mother's.

Silently, I slipped out of bed and, with exaggerated care, padded towards my bedroom door. I didn't feel any surprise at how calmly I acted. It felt like just another adventure, nothing for me to worry about. I approached the door and paused. Concealed in the darkness I listened, trying to understand what was happening.

From the room I heard a cry, quickly smothered — clearly my mother's. A gruff voice commanded her to be silent and to get the boy. The note of panic in the smothered cries rose as she begged to only take her and not to hurt me.

I could stand it no more and at thirteen years old I pulled open the door and strode into the hallway to defend my mother. In my mind I transformed into a knight from one of the many imaginary battles I fought in the castle. Still I felt no fear, only anger at this intrusion.

My strength and reflexes were incredible for my age, but physically I couldn't match even the smallest of the masked men who dragged my mother from her bed. Fearless, I charged the nearest, shouting with incoherent rage and striking him with my fists.

I heard the amusement in his voice as he laughed and casually backhanded me. The blow knocked me hard against the wall, forcing the breath from my lungs. Seeing me, my mother too began to struggle, but to no avail, held as she was between two of the men.

A fourth man, the last of the gang, angrily told the one that had just struck me to "stop pissing about and let's get the hell out of here". With a quick step he reached down and a single large hand grabbed my pyjama top and lifted me into the air. I struggled with all my might, punching and kicking at him as the others dragged my mother down the stairs. Despite my struggles I soon followed her.

The fourth man opened the door, checked the street outside with a quick glance before he waved to someone unseen outside. I bit the arm that held me, not enough to break the skin, but enough for him to cast me roughly to the ground. He kicked me, knocked the wind from me again and, using both hands this time, snatched me into the air.

At that moment something strange and wondrous occurred.

My mind burst free from the confines of my skull. With a roar that drowned out all other sound and like a battering ram I smashed into the head of the man that gripped me.

As I entered his mind I saw a kaleidoscope of images, what I later assumed to be the thoughts and memories of this man. He dropped me as he screamed and collapsed to his knees, clutching at the sides of his head. He then crumpled to the floor and fell silent.

At that same moment, I returned to my own head.

The other men stopped in surprise. My mother, still struggling, managed to break free and screamed as loudly as she could while crawling across the floor towards me. I have to admit, I was pretty shocked myself. I stared at the fallen man's face, and although it was covered in the woollen mask I watched a damp patch spreading.

In the distance a neighbour's dog barked and lights in other houses along the street flicked on. First one, and then more split the dark. The two men made a half hearted attempt at grabbing my mother, but in her panic she wrenched herself free. The fourth man quickly regained his composure. He muttered "this was some fucked up shit" before grabbing his two remaining men and pulling them into the street. I watched them leave, hearing the revving of an engine and squealing tyres as they made their escape.

My mother clutched at me, still sobbing, while I could only stare at the dead man's face. I had done that. I didn't know how I did it, but I had done that. And you know what? It didn't feel wrong.

The police arrived within minutes, summoned by one of the neighbours who looked warily through the open door before dialling 999. Gradually my mother calmed and by the time the ambulance arrived was able, in a stuttering voice, to answer some of their questions.

Over the next few days we learnt the whole story. The gang planned to kidnap her and use threats against me so she would open the bank doors early for them. They would then wait until the time lock opened the vault. Any staff that arrived for work would be taken hostage. Once the vault opened they'd clear out the cash and then be on their way. They'd already done this a few times in recent months. We were told that we had a lucky escape.

As for the dead man, his death was deemed to be from natural causes: a cerebral haemorrhage, but even after a post-mortem they couldn't determine the cause.

Chapter 6
Back in general population

Sunday lived up to its name as the guards escorted me back to the wing. A brisk wind chilled the skin, as befitting the time of year, but both the guard and I enjoyed the leisurely stroll. He noticed the Bible I carried as we passed through the security gates and into the wing itself. As I guessed it unlikely I'd get a library visit on a Sunday, I kept it for something to read once back in my cell. Pointing at the Bible. He told me that there would be a multi-denominational service later in the morning. I should just tell the officer supervising breakfast and I would be taken when it was time.

Now don't get me wrong, I don't swing that way, but a chance to get out of my cell and some company that wasn't on the other side of a steel door sounded like a pleasant diversion. Besides, the few days in the block had put me behind schedule on the plan. I needed to expand my contacts here in the prison. This would be a golden opportunity to do just that. I thanked him and said I would.

I really was feeling quite chipper that morning as I climbed the stairs back to my cell. It wasn't long before the door banged open again, and with my fellow convicts I was taken down to collect my breakfast. A few of my neighbours nodded in greeting and I saw no sign of

Peterson. Hopefully he still liked his food through a straw in the hospital wing.

Maybe it was the sun, or maybe just the good mood I was in, but I actually enjoyed that breakfast. It could be that the food for the block was given 'special' treatment making it even worse that the standard prison fare. No matter: I sat on my chair, a wooden one this time, and ate my breakfast with relish. My tea even had some sugar in it. Amazing how the simple pleasures can cheer you sometimes.

The service wouldn't start until eleven, so after handing my empty tray to the trustee I lay on the bed. It had only been four days, but just lying on a thin mattress in the daylight hours seemed such a luxury. I suppose I was easily pleased back then.

As eleven o'clock approached a few of us were taken from our cells and led back down to the security gate for the wing. There we waited to be taken to the chapel. I took the opportunity to get to know some of my neighbours.

First I spoke to the guy from the cell to my left, the one who masturbated while imagining his mother. Speaking to him you wouldn't believe he entertained such deviant desires, but he seemed amiable enough. We shook hands in a brisk, manly fashion, I introduced myself and he did the same, although just his surname — Davis.

It's not considered good form to ask a person what they're in for, so I didn't ask. I took a quick peek inside his mind and saw that he was a drug dealer who sold some bad stuff to the wrong person. Unusually, the police actually followed up on it, so here he was. He'd already served five years and had at least another five to go.

We followed the guards out into the yard, and once again it was a pleasant feeling to stretch the legs. I chatted to another prisoner. A shy fellow, his real name was Matthews, but everyone called him Bungle. That seemed to fit: he was a big idiot bear of a man. They say it's the quiet ones you have to watch and in his case that was certainly true. Again I peeked and, while normally a man of his crimes would fit in the nonce category, he was oddball enough and — let's admit it — big enough not to be at risk because of this.

Delving into his mind seemed more like the plot from a bad movie than somebody's life. A necrophiliac, he started many years ago by digging up fresh corpses and then molesting them. The fresher the better, of course, but the buried were never quite fresh enough so he took to breaking into funeral homes and mortuaries. He managed to get away with this for a few years, before finally succumbing to the temptation of the freshest meat of all. He lacked some imagination in luring the prostitute somewhere out of the way, but what he did to her after the strangulation more than made up for it.

Still, it was giving into this temptation that got him caught. Some of the other girls had seen him and even with the most basic description he easily stood out in a line-up. Now here he was, and he'd served eight years so far. As a sex offender he'd experienced some trouble at the beginning, but being built like a bull and with a curious ability to ignore pain, he got through it and now had a reasonably easy life working in the library. Chatting to him I saw he was an easygoing chap — he promised to bring me some books when he next did his rounds. As a category A prisoner it turned out that I could not go to the library myself, but books would be provided for me, as long as I obeyed the rules.

The chapel was situated at the far side of the prison, next to the perimeter fence. It was inside an old building dating back to the Napoleonic wars. As we approached, I noticed some narrow slits near the ground. One of the other prisoners told me that they let the light in for the old cells deep in the bowels of the building. It was here that the most dangerous French prisoners of war were kept, although these cells were now used as storerooms for decaying paperwork.

I found the inside of the chapel gloomy: a stark contrast to the glorious sunshine outside. Fifty or so of us walked in and found seats. I settled myself at the front. Most prisoners try to avoid sitting with their backs so exposed, but for me it wasn't an issue. It took a few minutes for everyone to get settled and the prayer and hymn books to be handed out.

I took the time to look around, nod in welcome at anyone who caught my eye and observe my surroundings. My eyes soon accustomed themselves to the murky light and I saw that this was a chapel in name only. A table stood as an altar, but a clean white cloth betrayed its purpose. A small crucifix of the tortured Christ stood behind the make-shift altar and a free standing lectern completed the ensemble.

Near the altar and positioned by the doors stood the guards that escorted us here. They were watchful, but at ease, not expecting any trouble. While many of the convicts here didn't believe and just came to get out of their cells, they did respect the service as a peaceful time for all concerned.

Flanked by another guard, the priest walked in and stepped up behind the altar. He saw me and faltered for a moment. Now this was interesting. I required no invitation and dived straight in. Immediately I discovered two items of interest. His first thought was that he knew me — no, that's not quite right. He didn't know who I was, but he did identify something about me. As if he knew what I was. I tried to push in further, to learn more from this thought, but it was a slippery thing and it eluded me.

The second thing that caught my attention was the pool of guilt that permeated his every thought and memory. This was too pervasive to escape and with ease I flicked through his memories like a photo album. His every dirty secret lay bare before me. If his flock knew what he was hiding, who he had protected, the sheep would soon turn to wolves.

I smiled. This was useful information. Revealing this would be a fine trigger for a riot, but I didn't need that for today. For the moment I enjoyed the priest's discomfort.

Only a few seconds passed as the priest and I stared at each other and you don't survive long in here without knowing when something was wrong. A few of the prisoners started to get restless. This wasn't the time, so I withdrew, and as I did so I felt eyes upon me. I turned to face them and saw a guard regarding me closely. He didn't seem angry, or agitated, but just watched.

He stood tall, towering above even the impressively sized Bungle. From his bearing I guessed he was ex-forces, but it was his look that that gave me pause. Then again, why should I hesitate? I had nothing to fear from this man, no matter his stature. So for the second time in as many minutes I invaded another person's mind.

Instantly I noticed the contrast. The priest's mind had been a storm of guilt and fear, this guard's only a serene calm. His name was David Hammond and I had guessed correctly about him being ex-forces. From his memories I gleaned visions of his combat tours with the Royal Marines in far flung desert places. He had seen action and lots of it. As a sniper he dealt death from afar. The weirdest part wasn't that he knew that I was there, but that he didn't mind. He looked me clean in the eye and invited me straight in.

His mind struck me as unlike anything I had previously experienced. I had encountered calm people before, but usually there was an undercurrent, some inner turmoil that boiled beneath their own understanding. Not this man, though. On all levels he was at peace with himself. No lingering doubts, no inner turmoil.

I don't mind admitting that I was shocked. I have been inside many minds and this knowing acceptance was unlike anything ... And there, in the centre I discovered it. I'm not sure what it was, but it was there, a solid beacon, a rock of light that anchored him.

I wanted to press closer, to peel away at this mystery, but the crowd was growing restless. All they could see was this guard, already a known entity within the prison — one of the few officers who received their respect — and me, staring at each other. They could almost taste the atmosphere between us. There was a palpable tension rising, so I calmly nodded at him in acknowledgement, winked at the priest, and settled back into my chair to watch him stutter his way through the service.

Chapter 7
Getting to know you

My mother and I took a two week break from work and school after the attack, but to be honest I think we were both glad to get back to our respective lives once the time was over. We loved each other dearly, but never really felt comfortable in each other's company for too long. We both appeared to recover quickly from what had happened, and neither of us felt depressed or anxious. We took a break, rested up and then got on with things.

Of course, I became an instant celebrity when I returned to school. Everybody wanted to hear the juicy details. I have to admit I was a little discomforted by the attention, but there was a certain thrill to it as well. Within days, though, it became old news and everything went back to normal. I faded once more into the background and that was just how I liked it.

I realised I possessed a gift. I knew that I had caused what happened to that man. Somehow, I killed him. Without touching him I killed him. So I started to explore it. By then I had turned thirteen, so that wasn't all I began exploring. I'm sure you catch my meaning.

At first I had little success and didn't seem to be able to do anything out of the ordinary. Whatever it was, I couldn't find a way to trigger it.

My newly developed interest in girls provoked the first intentional success. Like all boys I found it difficult to talk to the opposite sex. Well, not exactly talking to them, but knowing whether I should be talking to them or not. It was odd — I never suffered from a lack of confidence in anything else, but when I approached a girl I suddenly found myself worrying about whether she wanted to talk to me or not. I'd get caught up on worrying and then mutter something clumsy before beating a hasty retreat. This went on for a few months until I noticed Andrea.

Andrea moved into the area and started at my school that week. For a few days I only cast furtive glances at her and I wasn't the only one. She was a creature divine in schoolgirl form. She had the perfect shape and had the most delicious lips: probably an odd thing to fixate on, but that was the first thing I noticed about her. She really did have luscious lips, I just wanted to kiss them and taste them. For those few days I wrestled with myself, desperately attempting to think of something witty that would capture her attention.

That Friday afternoon, as everyone sat bored while listening to Mr Carroll drone on about the agricultural revolution it happened. As usual I had been sneaking peeks, you know, admiring the shape of her face, the swell of her breasts and imagining the delights hidden beneath the grey school uniform — and she looked at me. I was too slow to look away and for a moment our eyes met and in that moment I saw myself. It seems trite looking back on it now, but I saw myself through her eyes. I could hear her thoughts. I could feel what she felt. And luckily for me, she seemed to like what she saw.

After the bell rang and everyone made good their escape, I lingered and approached her. Like a gentleman I escorted her home and we talked. Well I mostly listened, but there was no worry about whether I should say the right thing or not because I could see what she wanted to hear before I even opened my mouth.

We dated for the rest of spring term, nothing serious, we were both still too young. But I still revelled in the glow of it all. Young love is a grand thing. Even now I can look back on that memory with fondness.

I showed her my secret places around the town, quiet places where we could kiss and fumble undisturbed. With her hand she gave me my first orgasm and at that exact moment something new occurred. That exquisite explosion of release somehow burst free from me into her and she orgasmed with me, without even being touched.

It's funny looking back. That first orgasm felt like nothing I have ever experienced since. Just like that first high with a drug, you can never quite reach that same feeling again, no matter how hard you try. Maybe that is what life is, the constant quest to regain what we once had, but can never feel again?

Young we may have been, but we did develop closeness, an intimacy that also aided the development of my abilities. My mind became entwined with hers and I eventually discovered that I could implant impulses of my own into her mind. At first it was just minor things, like when she felt disappointed at the present I had given her for her birthday. With a simple thought I turned that frown the right way up.

Later I used that influence in more significant ways. I heard the older boys talking about blow jobs and how amazing they felt. That sounded like something I wanted to experience for myself. Unfortunately Andrea was reluctant. I planted the impulse and she performed what I wanted, but while the impulse was enough to compel her, it wasn't enough to forestall the feelings of disgust and shame she felt afterwards.

Not surprisingly that marked the beginning of the end. She knew something wasn't right and while she didn't quite fear me, she did begin feeling disquiet when we were together. We lost that close companionship we once shared. I used my ability to prolong things, but my heart wasn't in it. I'd grown bored of her and although we hadn't gone all the way I now felt that for my first time I deserved something special — and quite frankly, Andrea no longer seemed special to me.

Despite her tears when we broke up, I think she was relieved deep down inside. I could have made it easier for her, but I did not.

Time rolled by and I would have to say that it was probably the best time of my life. It may sound like a cliché, but that made it no less true. I lived in a comfortable home, was well provided for. As long as I didn't get into trouble my mother didn't concern herself with what I did. She earned a good living, so I received a decent allowance. With my ability I could convince people to give me things if I wanted them anyway.

School for me back then was pure fun. My intelligence allowed me to breeze through the academic work. The larger boys no longer troubled me, not that they had very often anyway. Now I could also rely on more than my wits and my fists in the event of trouble. With some, I used an impulse to draw their attention onto someone else to torment. With others I let the fight happen, allowing my superior physical attributes to shine. If I looked like losing the fight a quick impulse would swing things back in my favour.

Amongst the other children I gained a reputation. They thought me a little creepy. They didn't know why, but they knew enough to keep their distance, unless I wanted them close and then they couldn't resist. I flirted with some of the girls, enjoying the odd encounter, but I became precious about my virginity. I knew what I wanted, but hadn't determined how I could achieve it. There are plenty of interesting diversions without having sex and with my talent there was always somebody who would indulge me.

With adults I experienced less of a problem. For the most part they weren't as sensitive as children. While some no doubt thought me an odd character, I did well at school and rarely got in trouble so didn't attract any undue attention. Another frustrating factor was that my abilities didn't seem to work as well with adults. Their minds were not as open and I found that I couldn't really get inside. I could glimpse their surface thoughts, but nothing deeper or hidden.

A year passed before I finally decided how and with whom I would lose my virginity. It amuses me now looking back at how seriously I took it, but back then it was almost a religious thing. As if it was a ritual that I had to complete to perfection.

The key to it all were the adults. I needed to bend one to my will. In return I would not just give myself to any girl, but to a woman. At the tender age of fourteen, this was my Everest. I know, I know, don't judge me. We're all young once.

Ms Clarke presented that opportunity. Ms Clarke taught English Literature. Even now I stand to attention thinking about her. She was perfect in every way, in her late twenties, her beautiful face framed with raven dark hair.

Her body was full in ways the girls around me were not. And her silk stocking clad legs were simply amazing.

I also knew that she was the secret fantasy of many of the boys at the school, and more than one would drop his pencil so they could try and peek up her skirt. I remember once her breast brushed my shoulder as she leaned over me to comment on my work.

I think it was that lightest of caresses that sealed the deal for me.

Adult minds still presented a mystery to me and so during every lesson with her I focused on her. With all my will I attempted to break into her mind, to uncover what secrets that lay beneath her surface thoughts. I enjoyed no success at first, but I did develop the knack of multi-tasking with my school work and mental assault.

In the end two arguing children provided the breakthrough I needed. When I saw them arguing in the playground I thought it would be fun for them to settle their differences once and for all.

I had never tried sending impulses to more than one person at a time and naturally it proved harder than I anticipated, but not impossible. As I got used to separating the conflicting thoughts and emotions it grew easier. While I watched them fight it out I realised that this is how adults were different.

It seemed to me that with children their thoughts are all on the same level: they don't necessarily raise one thought or feeling above another. They also focused more, the form of their thoughts and emotions simpler so that it was easier for me to penetrate. Adults have thoughts firing all over the place, and more importantly on different levels. Their surface thoughts I could already read — it was the maelstrom underneath that blocked my access. If I treated the adult mind like many children's minds then maybe I could force a way in.

In the lesson the next day I tested my theory and after an initial struggle it worked. Ms Clarke looked at me with those full lips of hers and when I smiled, she smiled back. I had done it. I had successfully subverted a mind more developed than my own.

Chapter 8
Life in the slow lane

The court case wouldn't begin for several weeks so I had to bide my time and allowed myself to slip into the routine of prison life. As a category A remand prisoner I wasn't permitted to join a work detail. This meant that I spent most of each day alone in my cell. Bungle came through for me and provided a steady stream of books. As you can imagine, I read a lot in that time.

I found it quite frustrating. I hadn't expected to be locked up for so much of the day. To plant my suggestions I really needed to mingle with as much of the population, both guards and prisoners, as I could.

Still, most days provided a couple of social opportunities, the brief exercise period in the morning and then association time in the evening. Exercise was held in the yard outside the wing. The cold weather had now drawn in, but despite the cold it was good to walk in the open air and chat with the other prisoners.

There was the option of going to the gym instead of the yard, but I've never needed any help in keeping fit and the guards watched us more closely in the gym. The yard had fewer guards and provided more opportunities for discreet conversation.

The association periods in the evening lasted only for an hour but did provide more time for me to get chatting with the others. Unfortunately these didn't occur every day. With so many category A prisoners we were only allowed out in small groups. An old television hung in one corner of the hall where we mingled. The choice for viewing was quite limited and we couldn't switch the channels, so it was usually Eastenders or some other dross on screen. Not the sort of thing I liked to watch, but it was oddly popular with the other inmates. I guess watching anything is better than staring at a cell wall.

As well as the TV a few tables lined one wall with various games like chess, draughts and cards we could play. I'd not really played chess as a child, but found that I liked it and appeared to have a natural talent for it. I will confess that it's quite a bit easier if you know what moves your opponent was about to play. Still I rarely used my abilities as I enjoyed the challenge of it. I discovered a purity to the game which appealed to me. There was no chance involved. The only random elements were the people playing.

Those short hours each day helped break the monotony of the daily routine and also enabled me to get to know my fellow prisoners better. It was vital for me to know who was capable of what, who could be relied upon and who would need more convincing.

For the remaining twenty two hours a day I stayed locked in my cell. As well as reading I spent considerable time thinking of my plan and I eventually realised that I had miscalculated. I wasn't worried about the impending court battle as I didn't need to worry about the actual case. I did not expect to win. I only wanted to put on a memorable show.

The final stand in the prison was another matter. I had not realised how separate the different parts of the prison were. It would be easy to seize the wing, but for my last stand I wanted something much more visible — something so big it couldn't be hidden away. For that to be certain I would have to take over the whole prison.

I used my limited time and contact with the prisoners to good effect. When I decided to act most of them would be with me: some through their natural inclinations, others through the impulses I planted in their minds. When the time came those impulses would trigger and they would do what was needed.

I followed the same routine with the guards, but here I encountered a problem. Officer Hammond took too much of an interest in me. I needed to subvert the guards to be able to seize control of the whole prison. If I was unable to seal the main gates, reinforcements could rapidly be brought in and my insurrection quickly crushed. More importantly, without the contact with the outside world it could be stopped quietly and without the fanfare I yearned for.

Officer Hammond interfered with this plan. He was always present and watching me closely. He interrupted me as I conversed with the other guards and his very presence proved to be a disruptive influence. I had no idea how he did it, but my impulses appeared to be weakened by his proximity.

I attempted a more direct approach with him, once again entering his mind. As before he allowed me to enter without any resistance. He let me see whatever I wanted: his childhood memories, his postings with the marines even the little thoughts he kept hidden from himself. It did no good. I could do nothing with them. There was no give in him. I tried introducing new thoughts, to disrupt his usual thinking, to probe for some weakness. Nothing worked. The alien thoughts wouldn't fit into his mindscape. The rock that anchored his thinking would not budge.

It soon became clear that I needed to get him out of the way. The mental attack simply wasn't working, so that left a physical assault. Tempting as it was to do it personally I didn't need that complication just yet. Luckily I had plenty of willing volunteers to hand.

The attack took place while we were being locked back into our cells. Three prisoners from the neighbouring did the deed, two grabbing him from either side as the third moved in with a knife. Hammond responded quickly, taking one down before being stabbed in the arm. He felled the other trying to hold him with a savage blow to the temple. The third attacker stabbed him in the stomach before reinforcements arrived. It was with some relief I watched him fall, clutching his wound.

With Hammond out of the way I stepped up my campaign seeding more impulses into the guards' minds. Two days later, while lying in my cell, the door opened and Hammond stood there. He smiled coldly as he informed me that my court date had been set and that I would attend in three days for the trial to begin.

His smile dropped as he turned to leave, I saw his eyes narrow as he said, "Nice try by the way". He then left me to my thoughts.

Chapter 9
The first court appearance

My day in court finally arrived and I don't mind admitting that I felt quite excited. No stage fright for me — I wanted to get this party started! I struggled to contain that excitement as I rushed through breakfast. I then had to impatiently wait for the guards to process my transfer. I didn't want to alert the guards by appearing too happy at attending my trial.

I'd return the same day, but any movement had to be monitored and the proper forms completed. It took some arranging, but an old friend organised a new suit for the occasion. It felt good to be out of the prison denims and into something more stylish. I looked as dapper as possible considering the circumstances. I find it's always important to make a good first impression.

A private security firm provided transport to court. They loaded us into the back of a white lorry. Once inside, they ushered us into individual cells: each one tiny, with just enough room to sit on the hard plastic seat. A window of armoured glass provided a tiny portal to the world outside. It was positioned too high to see through while sitting, so I stood for most of the journey. Many weeks had passed since I last saw anything beyond the confines of the prison, and I enjoyed the view as we crawled through the early morning traffic.

It occurred to me that escaping would be easy. But then I could have escaped the prison just as easily.

We arrived at the courthouse and unloaded from the lorry. The guards then escorted us into the underground holding facility beneath the old building. I amused myself by reading some of the scrawled graffiti while I waited.

After an hour I was walked upstairs into the courtroom itself. I sat in the dock, flanked by two guards. Two policemen stood by the main doors as additional security. I savoured the moment and casually looked around. The courtroom was spacious but without windows. I smelt the history of the place — many people had received their justice here for many years and now it was my turn. I couldn't wait!

Across from me, empty for the moment, was the bench where the judge would preside. Below me, at the desks for the lawyers, the prosecution lawyer and his assistants talked quietly amongst themselves. The desk for the defence team was of course vacant. To my right stood the witness box, also empty for the moment. Further away, on my left, two more benches filled with the jurors for my case.

The jury was a mix of both sexes. I sensed that some of them knew of me, a few did not. Naturally I took a little dip inside their minds. Some were thrilled with the chance to decide another's fate. Others looked nervous and would much rather be about the normal lives.

Well, they would be in for something special. If only they knew how lucky they were!

Behind and above me loomed the public gallery. The seats already filled with reporters, all clutching tablets, waiting eagerly for something juicy to report.

After a few minutes the judge made his grand appearance. He wore his full finery, red robe and white wig. Everyone stood up as he entered, and I did likewise. Now wasn't the time to miss the little niceties.

Once the judge sat down, everyone else did the same. We then went through the initial proceedings. I confirmed my identity when asked. The many charges were all read out individually. That took a while, but the important ones were the murder of three passers-by and the two police officers who responded to the panicked 999 calls. Then they asked me how I pleaded.

I replied that my guilt or otherwise wasn't for me to decide and that I'm sure the jury would let me know one way or the other soon enough. The judge fixed me with a baleful glare, although a couple of the jurors and reporters could be heard chuckling nervously. At least somebody appreciated my wit. He instructed the court recorder to write my plea as not guilty.

He then asked whether I still refused legal counsel, I confirmed that I did and that I wouldn't need a lawyer to present the truth. Again he frowned at me before declaring that it was my choice, and that I wouldn't be able to appeal on the grounds that I hadn't been represented. I shrugged and replied that there would be no need for me to appeal. He frowned again. From his surface thoughts I read that he was very unhappy about this. People that represented themselves always caused trouble as they didn't know how things worked. He was right about that, but not in the way he imagined.

I was told to sit back down and then it was the prosecution's turn. The prosecutor stood, ready to begin his case against me.

Looking at him I slipped effortlessly into his mind. I felt how pleased he was. This was a high profile case, my guilt was clear and this would progress his career nicely. I focused past these surface thoughts, through the stuff under the surface about his wife, his mistress and his children. I dug deeper, below the growing hunger, his need for a coffee and a good smoke. I forced my way deeper still, to the thoughts that were no longer thoughts, but the primitive impulses that governed his body.

I found the triggers I wanted and pushed. The prosecutor started to speak and without warning choked on his words. A low moan escaped his lips as he stumbled forward and collapsed across his papers. I laughed out loud as one of the police officers rushed to his aid. I roared with laughter as the officer gave CPR. Normally his swift actions would have saved the lawyer's life, but not today. He didn't have a chance, especially as I kept pushing at those triggers, ensuring that his breathing would not restart.

With a contended sigh I stopped laughing. The second police officer spoke into his radio and then there was a hush throughout the courtroom. "I hope the prosecution has a stronger case than that," I said, and chuckled again.

The judge's anger finally broke through his control. "You will be silent! You will remain silent unless given leave to speak and you will show the proper respect to the officers of this court. If you do not, you will be held in contempt of court."

"Contempt of court?" I asked in reply. "My opinion of this court is not what you should be worried about." I chuckled again. "And you —" I pointed at him, "— cannot stop this."

From behind me I heard the frantic scribble of pencils upon paper. I smiled again. We were off to a good start.

The judge's face darkened with fury, and he ordered the guards to take me back to the cells. The trial would resume the next morning. The guards escorted me from the dock, but before I left I looked up at the public gallery, gave them my best smile, and allowed myself to be taken below.

As I was led away the paramedics arrived and started their futile attempts to revive the prosecutor.

Chapter 10
Then there was just me

While it lasted, the affair with Ms Clarke provided pleasure I'd previously only imagined. I finally lost my virginity in the bedroom of her cosy flat. The experience proved better than I anticipated. I was right to have waited. Her body looked so much fuller than those of the girls at the school, and her greater experience marked her as a more meaningful prize than any of those schoolgirls could have been.

She introduced me to a range of delights, although not as willingly as I would have liked. I enjoyed total control. My mastery over her mind had quickly developed. That skill enabled me to develop my ability with other adults, but for two glorious months Ms Clarke became my sole focus and obsession.

As an adolescent I naturally saw the affair as something deeper than it really was. I was young. I even fancied that I fell in love for a time. With 20/20 hindsight I now see that lust, not love, drove my passions. Nothing wrong with that: the sex was quite simply fantastic. Her age meant she was experienced enough to be exotic, but her body still young enough to be alluring. The memories fill me with a warm feeling even now.

Unfortunately the affair didn't end well. I learnt the valuable lesson of discretion, but it was a close call. I'll hold my hand up and admit that it was all my fault. I couldn't help but show off.

I bragged about my conquest and even convinced her to show some of what made her special to me in class. Unsurprisingly word soon spread. It took a frantic effort for me to prevent word reaching my mother. A lot of minds needed persuasion which taxed my fledgling talent to the limit. Unfortunately for Ms Clarke she lost her job, but I did manage to prevent the reason becoming public knowledge. I'm certain she found another job.

For the remainder of my time at school I kept my nose clean. I still delved into people's minds if I wanted to know something, or needed something to happen, but I did learn to be more considered about the whole thing. The Headmistress knew that somehow I had pulled a fast one on her and watched me like a hawk. So I got on with my studies and as I approached the age of sixteen I had to make the same decision all the other teenagers had to make. What would my future entail?

On that day I attended the career guidance interview. I had no idea what I wanted to do with my life, but who does at that age? I did have an interest in computers, but they were new enough then that there was no clear route to a career in that direction. Another option was my childhood passion for astronomy. Her advice was run of the mill. I should stay on at sixth form, or go to college and stick with academic studies for a few years, pass my A-levels, then study for a degree. It seemed like a reasonable plan. I was sure I could get through these studies as easily as I had at school. She advised me to speak with my parents and I said I would do so.

A normal day, nothing at all exciting or interesting about it.

As usual I arrived home before my mother. She would generally return around six in the evening, then cook dinner for us both that we ate watching TV. I wasn't too concerned when she didn't arrive at the usual time. Sometimes she worked late, although she would normally call if that was the case. When she still hadn't returned a few hours later I started to worry.

The sudden knock at the door startled me.

Opening the door I looked up at the policeman. I didn't need any special gift to predict what he was about to say. One look was enough to see the well practised words forming on his lips. There had been a terrible accident, he was very sorry, but I had to come with him. As the only living relative it was my duty to identify the body. He didn't know the details, only that it had been a road traffic accident.

My first ride in a police car was to go and see my mother's body. I don't think I really understood what had happened until I stood before the trolley. A white clad assistant pulled back the sheet and I saw her face. It didn't look too bad, some cuts and bruising. Not enough to have killed her, but there she lay, cold and still. I didn't even realise I was crying.

I encountered Mr Roberts, the portly bank manager, waiting at the hospital. He witnessed the accident and accompanied her in the ambulance. He told me that she had died on the journey. He didn't want to tell me the details, but he did in the end — I needed to know. I must have been in shock. I didn't even consider just pulling it from his head.

I tried to make sense of it. He told me what he witnessed: a silver car coming too fast as she crossed the road. Too late the driver tried to swerve, to no avail. I later discovered he had been drunk at the wheel.

I wasn't old enough to be left in my own care, but Mr Roberts let me stay with him until all the details had been worked out. He made the funeral arrangements, helped me pick out the clothes she would wear, the coffin she would lie in. He covered all the costs and while he tried his best, he really couldn't help my anguish. Only one person had ever helped me when I felt lost or frightened and she was no longer there.

Time passed in a confused blur and all too quickly the day of the funeral arrived. I don't really remember much of it. There was a service, the priest telling us that she was a great woman, how everybody had loved her. I loved her. I didn't know these other people. I don't think I have ever loved anybody else and I know now that I will never do so again. I stood, trying to be strong, but not quite a man. I felt like a little boy.

My ability proved less than helpful. Along with my own grief, I absorbed the sorrow of all those around me. Not in an empathic sense, their grief flooded with my own, drowned my being. I never realised how popular she was, how well liked. I didn't know any of these people, but here they were: all saying goodbye, and their grief only magnified my own.

After an eternity the service ended. Some of those strangers approached me. They offered their condolences. I accepted them as best I could. I thanked them for attending. Some became distraught, and I found myself trying to comfort them, to send an impulse with calm. That was a mistake. My thoughts came from my own bottomless sorrow and they helped no-one.

We were driven to the graveyard, but the headstone wasn't laid. Just the hole in the ground edged with artificial grass. It looked deep, like a permanent wound in the earth. They lowered her into that earthen pit. I couldn't stop the cry that escaped me. People tried not to look at me.

Eventually the ordeal ended, the people left, returned to their own lives, taking their sadness with them. Mr Roberts and I returned to his home, barely speaking, not knowing one another. Neither of us was able to bring any comfort to the other. He drank alone, found some small solace in the fine whiskey that he drank. He offered me a glass, but I had no taste for it. There was no escape for me that way.

In time my grief hardened, became a bitter, cold thing. I buried it deep inside, kept it hidden from the world. Finally after two months I hunted the driver down. It wasn't easy — no-one seemed to know who he was or where he lived. I couldn't get close to the people who knew so I could pluck it from their heads. In the end I encountered a young reporter who gave me what I needed, and that evening I walked to the house of Martin Cox.

In those days, drink driving wasn't considered the serious crime that it is today. Even with a fatality he remained free until the trial. And then he might only receive a few years. It didn't seem a fair punishment. These days he would already be in prison and that might have saved him.

For hours I watched him with his family. From his thoughts and theirs, I discovered what had happened. He turned to drink to drown his guilt, the usual clichéd story. It started with a few drinks occasionally after work, soon becoming every evening. Then at lunch times, then slowly starting earlier each day until finally he drank from the moment he woke. He almost destroyed his own family. His wife and their two children had been on the verge of leaving him. Killing my mother shocked him sober. He slowly began to put his life back on track, to rebuild the connections with his family. It should have provided some solace for me that some good had emerged from my mother's death. But it didn't. All I saw was the man who killed my mother being rewarded for it.

For a time I watched them, this family reborn from my mother's blood. Their renewed happiness tainted by his guilt. Before arriving I thought that it would be an easy thing to snuff out the life that caused me such pain, but the sight of this family together gave me pause. Was I right to perform the deed I had planned?

Over the past weeks I had imagined this moment. I pictured the terrible vengeance that I would wreak upon this man and those closest to him. I would destroy all that he loved and when that was done I would destroy him. Some part of me knew this wouldn't make things right. I could hear my mother's voice: "Two wrongs don't make a right".

I continued to observe and if I had just walked away then maybe everything would now be different. I didn't walk away. I stood, shrouded in the shadows, and the icy rage inside me grew. It demanded vengeance. Why should this man live? The bitterness coiled within me, insistent with its fury.

His family left, and delving into their thoughts I learned they would be gone until the next day. I waited for a few more minutes then approached the house and knocked on the door. I said nothing as he opened the door, then my mind smashed into his. He staggered backwards from the force. He recognised me, and I suddenly remembered him from the funeral. He had lurked in the distance, a furtive presence that remained only for a few moments. The thought of him being there angered me further. The darkness within me overpowered him. I listened to him beg for forgiveness, that he hadn't meant to hurt anybody.

His pleas infuriated me. I barely heard them as I ripped through his memories. From his hidden thoughts I located a stashed bottle of cheap spirits, with his hands I poured a drink. He cried out, louder now as I forced him to drink it. He finished the first glass, half of the clear liquid spilled down his chest.

My will forced him to pour another. He continued to beg me not to do this. He drank the second glass, the warmth of the drink started to fill him. I sensed his shame as he felt the pang of pleasure at its taste. I almost revelled in it as he drank the third measure. His demon thirst awakened, inflamed as he swallowed another mouthful.

A fourth generous measure, then a fifth emptied the bottle. Gripping the drained glass with one hand he smashed it against the table. Only then did he understand the reality of his doom. He took the broken glass and cut into his arm. The blood sprang free as if eager for release. He continued to plead with me as he cut again, deeper this time. The glass was slick, but he managed to hold on to it as he cut again.

I stayed with him as the blood drained and his mind faded. He slipped away into the abyss and I almost went with him as he fell deeper into the darkness. The glass dropped to the floor. I left the house, closing the door with my foot, and walked into the night.

Chapter 11
Second day in court

As with the previous day I looked forward to another interesting hearing, but this time I had something different planned. Despite my impatience proper procedure had to be followed and it took a few hours to travel from my cell to the court. The court room sounded noticeably busier that morning, much noisier than the day before. The public gallery filled to bursting with reporters. Apparently yesterday's events had sparked considerable interest. I vowed to make sure that they would not leave disappointed. I almost tasted their anticipation for juicy copy.

The judge entered the room. We all rose to our feet and did not sit until he did. Before the proceedings began, he warned me sternly that I would behave correctly and show the court the proper respect. With a practised expression of innocence I assured him that I would. He repeated his invitation for proper legal counsel, which I again refused. With that we started.

We welcomed a new prosecutor, a middle-aged woman cursed with a sharp face. She smoothed her gown primly as she stood. Hopefully she possessed stronger lungs than the last rather weak specimen. I smiled at the thought. She introduced her case by summarising my crimes, describing the terrible things that I committed on that winter morning. Some of the jurors seemed a little upset by the graphic detail, but she comforted them with the promise of evidence that would prove my guilt beyond a shadow of a doubt. She paused, letting the descriptions settle in the jurors' imaginations, then summoned her first witness.

The witness entered: one of the armed response team officers who arrived on the scene shortly after I murdered his colleagues. He held the bible in one hand and swore to tell the truth, the whole truth and nothing but the truth. The prosecutor stepped up to the witness stand and asked him to confirm his identity.

He tried to reply, he really did, but I wouldn't let him. Once more he tried, but his mouth couldn't form the words. From across the courtroom we heard only mumbling. These incoherent mumbles make no sense and they rose sharply in pitch as he became frantic. The judge attempted to help him, telling the officer, resplendent in his uniform, to calm down and reply to the prosecutor's questions. This time he turned red in the face as he strained to answer, but once again I refused to permit him.

After several minutes of cajoling, followed by stern commands they gave up and summoned the second witness. An elderly lady tottered slowly to the stand. I remembered her accompanying her friend before I brutally snatched that friend's life away. She glared at me with a mixture of defiance and fear. The prosecutor approached the witness stand and after the old lady recited the oath asked her to confirm her identity. In a clear voice she stated that her name was Gillian Travers.

Encouraged by this progress the prosecutor prompted her to describe the events she had witnessed. Before she could speak I delved inside her, and together we relived the grim scene. I forced the memory into a loop and together we watched it again and again. At first she remained stoically silent, but after several repetitions she began to tremble and eventually to weep. They were tiny sobs, pathetic really, but they carried across the room. I heard gasps of sympathy around me and smiled. Over and over she watched her friend murdered, the scene framed by my happy grin. She couldn't see me through her tears, but she felt my gaze and she knew that somehow I was in there with her.

The prosecutor attempted to calm the poor woman, but sadly to no avail. In the end a court official led her from the room. Her exit trailed by the sympathies of everybody else in the court. As she left and the door closed behind her I released her from my grasp and relaxed to await the next witness.

The court filled with the murmur of hushed conversation. Everyone realised something was very wrong. The judge called a short recess and instructed the prosecutor to check her witnesses, to make sure they were ready to give their evidence.

All morning they tried, but no-one could talk. They all identified themselves and swore the oath then said no more. The jurors and press in the public gallery grew ever more restless. They didn't know what they were witnessing, but they were sure that this wasn't how it was supposed to work.

I felt some relief when lunchtime arrived. Taking such direct control of people proved a lot more effort than my preferred method of implanting thoughts over time. My head pounded and I barely tasted the sandwiches provided for lunch. The short break revived me somewhat and I felt restored when the afternoon session resumed.

The prosecutor changed tactics. She was getting nowhere with the witnesses so she switched to presenting the physical evidence. First she showed the court crime scene photos of the street where it occurred. She laid it on thick, and after displaying the pictures of the bodies she played the CCTV footage of the attacks.

There I stood, the star of this grainy footage, slumped on the pavement, dressed in rags. I hardly recognised myself. One moment sitting, swaddled in dirty blankets, the next upright. The blankets then pooled at my feet. The court watched me kill three passers-by and the two police first responders with brutal efficiency. Some thought it quite exciting and drew hushed comment. The next bit admittedly was a bit boring, just me sitting there waiting for the armed response team. The civilised person that I am, I surrendered to them and the footage ended. Naturally they didn't show the video of me receiving a beating in the van, but no matter.

I let her finish her little presentation. The photos only caught the aftermath and the video was nowhere near clear enough to identify me with any certainty. I decided that it was time to get the witnesses back in. I raised my hand like a child in class and said, "This show and tell is all very well, but it isn't evidence of what I may or may not have done."

She knew I was right, although she did a reasonable job at hiding it. She also knew that the witnesses needed to state what I had done. They had to point to me, and declare my guilt. But now she was concerned. She didn't know what had silenced all the witnesses that morning, but she guessed it had something to do with me. And now she worried why I want them back in the courtroom.

The judge reluctantly agreed, stating that the witnesses must provide their testimony — although he too was suspicious of my intent and, in fairness, he had good reason to be. They summoned the armed response officer back to the stand. My time in his mind had damaged his thoughts. Something had shaken loose, and he didn't remember all that he saw. From his memories I learned that an assistant had coached him on what to say. That was exactly what I needed for the day's grand finale.

The officer took the stand. Understandably he felt a little nervous. Once again he identified himself and recited the oath, but as soon as he completed it I interrupted. I addressed the court in general, musing on how binding this oath really is.

"How binding is this oath? Would he be punished by the court for lying if he gave evidence? My faith is not strong in the court punishing its own." With a snap of my fingers I laughed out loud. "I have it. If you break the oath, you die. Simple as that, you will die in that witness box if you don't speak the truth."

The judge's fury was a delight to behold.

"You will not threaten witnesses in my courtroom!"

Calmly I replied, "There is no threat. He took the oath and if God strikes him down for breaking it that would hardly be my doing."

The prosecutor and the witness both looked a little nervous about my little outburst, but they knew it had to be an act. They knew it was clearly bluster on my part and so they followed the prepared line as I assumed they would. They reached the part I knew had been coached and while it wasn't a lie, he didn't know if it was or not and she knew that he'd been manipulated for that testimony.

The words barely left his lips when he collapsed. One of the jurors screamed, and I watched the panicked rush to reach him. They needn't have bothered. He died before hitting the floor. For the second day in a row the court watched a wasted effort in resuscitation. The reporters loved it and scribbled excitedly in their notebooks.

I beamed a happy smile at the shocked prosecutor. "I did warn him. You had to push him though. You made the man lie and now you've killed him."

I turned to the judge. "One dead every day was my promise."

I wore that smile all the way back to the holding cells. The effort drained me but it was Friday so I had the weekend to recover for the next session. A whole weekend in which to rest and to dream of the coming entertainments.

Chapter 12
The great escape

Looking back I realised I had done wrong. Hell, I knew that the moment I killed him. My mother would never have wanted revenge, especially not in that way. Even in the moment itself I couldn't prevent what I forced him to do. I tried to move on. Even with that distraction I performed well in my exams and had been accepted into college for further studies. When the summer holidays ended I would start college.

I never made it.

Throughout the summer I searched for a means of escape, for something that would take the pain away. There was a great conflict inside me, the grief more so than guilt. In both cases I didn't know how to deal with it. My mother had been the only person that I ever talked to. Now there was no-one. I tried to talk to Mr Roberts, but as I edged onto the subject of what I did I sensed his mounting horror. Luckily he had already drunk a few whiskies and I easily scrubbed the memory from his mind. From that moment he always felt slightly uneasy in my company, without really knowing why.

While I couldn't admit it to myself at the time, with hindsight I can accept that I was more than a little afraid. I had killed a man: not in self defence like before, but in cold blood. I knew that revenge couldn't justify his murder. There would be consequences.

Like Mr Roberts I first tried drink to drown the pain, to find some way to smother the feelings. A numb oblivion would surely be better than the constant ache that never faded. I still had no taste for it, I didn't enjoy the act and while drinking enough brought escape for a few short hours, the pain would return even worse the next day. So my search continued.

A brilliant idea occurred to me one morning. Not unusually I felt more than a little worse for wear from the night before. It struck me that with my ability I could dump the pain onto others. Let them carry my grief and guilt — I would be free. After all, a problem shared is a problem halved. I tried it that very morning. I poured my grief and revulsion out into strangers as they walked by.

It didn't take me long to discover I would find no reprieve that way. My grief spilled out, but it had no end. No matter how much I poured into the people around me, there was always more. Forcing it on others brought no relief at all. All I created was a cloud of misery that polluted passers-by.

I became an observer, sitting alone in the park, just watching the world go by. Here I suffered a contradiction. I set myself apart from the world I watched. I existed as a poisoned thing, separate from the people around me. Yet for some short time it eased my troubles. I found it a balm to see others go about their lives, to know that joy existed in the world. Even if it would never be for me.

In the park I often encountered a small group of young people, a couple of whom I recognised from my year at school. On occasion they noticed me sitting alone and invited me to join their games. Always I declined and kept myself apart.

I continued to just watch them. I noticed something different about them that I couldn't quite place. Their behaviour seemed both over the top and forced, yet completely natural at the same time. They also rolled their own cigarettes and shared them with each other, something else I'd not seen before.

I know, pretty naive.

Finally I accepted their invitation. I reasoned that it couldn't make anything worse. So I joined their circle. Soon enough they rolled a smoke and after a couple of them smoked a few puffs, one of the girls offered it to me. At first I hesitated. I've never really had the urge to smoke, but something smelled funny and peering into their minds I saw a change. This difference to their minds intrigued me, so I smoked a drag. They laughed as I coughed my guts up, but in a good way. Undeterred I tried it again.

After a few turns around the group another a boy with a patchy beard rolled another joint. After smoking some more I experienced a pleasant feeling: my head felt light and fuzzy, almost separated from by body. I lay back in the grass, the sun on my face, thinking nothing and realised that I had forgotten my troubles. They seemed a world away.

I spent more time with my new friends, chilling out with them in the park. I also visited them in their homes in the evenings. I kept myself to myself, but they didn't mind the fact that I kept to the periphery. The smoking sessions in the evening differed from those during the day. In the park it was a light thing, getting a little stoned and having a bit of fun. In the evening it took on a serious tone, more intense, pushing to get high rather than just stoned.

Back then when you visited a dealer they offered a range of good stuff for you try. Different varieties each provided a different buzz or feeling. These days it's the same old soapbar or skunk. One night we tried something new. Whatever this hash was laced with, it was a little bit trippy and one of the girls suddenly freaked out.

We were all friends so everyone tried to help, but the more we crowded her, the more she freaked. I dipped into her mind and instantly saw the cause of her fear. At the corners of her vision, little crawly things nibbled and squirmed. I radiated calm and cleared the others away. I smothered her panic with the stoned joy that fogged my mind. This soothed her and eventually she calmed. We all then giggled like children for no real reason, just for the fun of it.

To my surprise I enjoyed that moment of sharing. Unlike when I poured my pain into strangers, there was a delight in sharing my joy with friends. I became well known as the dude to have a smoke with. Everyone always experienced a good buzz when they smoked with me. With the groups as a whole I could just let it wash out of me and into them all. With my ability I could take individuals and pushed their high to a new level.

I'd inherited a reasonable sum from my mother's will, so I left Mr Roberts' house. I think he felt relieved to see me go. I didn't go to college and instead spent my time in a pleasant fugue with like minded people. For a time I experienced no dark thoughts, I suppressed the grief and pushed it deep, enjoying the moment.

Chapter 13
Sunday morning blues

I continued to attend Sunday Mass each week. Annoyingly it proved the only regular avenue for contact with prisoners and guards from other wings in the prison. Faking some minor illnesses also allowed access to the hospital wing for a few short visits. If I was to seize the prison, this scant contact was essential for my plan to succeed. The fact that it provided a little extra time out of my cell was no bad thing, even if it did mean listening to the hypocritical sermons from the nervous priest. I rarely bothered to invade his mind any more. My presence alone unsettled him.

That Sunday proved no exception. With so little time remaining I needed to use every moment available. The walk to chapel wasn't as pleasant as it had been. The winter weather had definitely closed in and even wrapped up with our prison issue donkey jackets we still felt the bitter cold. As always we sat and waited for the priest to make his entrance. I spent the time filtering through the minds around me.

As I passed through each mind I planted more impulses. I'd inserted these at every opportunity. Each impulse planted a seed that lay in wait for the coming battle. Each one built on the previous seeds — they meshed together within the person's mind. When the time came these instructions would flower and the prisoner or guard would do whatever I commanded.

I remember how excited I felt, with the final battle so close. I estimated that at best the court case would last another week, probably less. They couldn't convict me; the evidence just wasn't strong enough. The question was, how long would they keep trying? They wouldn't release me either. I knew that much for certain. They couldn't prove my guilt, but they knew that they couldn't set me free. There's no shortage of legal tricks to keep a person locked up, even without a conviction.

Knowing that so little time remained for me was comforting. With the coming stand my name would become known and remembered. I really don't recall why that mattered so much. I suppose there's nothing wrong with going out with a bang.

I noticed the prisoners getting a little restless. Already much later than usual, the priest hadn't arrived. I contemplated the poor priest's future. I'm sure he would be the first to agree that you reap what you sow.

The next Sunday Mass would be the start of something terrible and wonderful. He would be right at the epicentre when it all kicks off. It couldn't happen to a nicer person, I thought to myself with a small grin.

Officer Hammond entered, and as always his presence marred my happy thoughts. I hadn't figured out how he interfered with my ability. He couldn't block me planting the impulses, but he did weaken their potency. He couldn't stop the plan. He *mustn't* stop the plan. My instinct warned me that he represented an unneeded risk. It would be wise for me to remove him before the final event — yes, very wise indeed, even if that did mean losing a few pawns.

Hammond positioned himself next to the altar and stood there, impassive. He paid me some extra attention as he scanned the crowd. I didn't feel flattered. Something did not feel right at that moment.

A priest walked in behind and he was a complete stranger to me. I'm no expert, but I could see that he was dressed differently. Not a priest at all — maybe a monk? If so, this represented something new. I cast my mind out, eager to unravel this new person and learn his secrets.

My mind bounced off him.

Impossible!

I tried again, more carefully this time, but again some barrier prevented my mind's entrance. I had never experienced anything like this before. Since my teenage years I could always enter another's mind. Naturally some were more difficult than others, but there's always been a way in. He stepped up to the altar and introduced himself as Friar Francis. He came as a replacement for our regular priest. Who had unfortunately been taken ill. He hoped that we could all find space for the sick priest in our prayers.

I tried again, more forcefully this time. I gathered my will and unleashed it in a violent surge at his skull. Still I failed to gain admittance. I tried again, this time grappling with his mind, but I found no purchase. My mind slipped from his like wet glass.

This Friar looked straight at me. His face appeared serene, contrasting with the hardness in his eyes. Like the ex-marine standing beside him, he had witnessed things. He stood before me, tall and gaunt, dressed in the black robes of his order. And he smiled at me. I sensed no warmth in that look. It was a knowing smile, a challenging smile.

I changed tactics and delved into Hammond's mind. I slipped in easily and felt some relief. At least my talent still worked. I tore through his memories seeking some connection with this monk. I found the link I sought and followed the thread. It led me to the rock at the centre of his being and I could follow no further.

With a feeling of some disquiet I withdrew. Hammond nodded to the Friar and the mass began. All I could do was watch and listen. I tried to salvage some of my wasted effort and resumed planting impulses in the minds around me. I barely contained my fury as I watched the seeds melt away as soon as I planted them.

This was not a good start to the day.

I began to worry that maybe, just maybe, I needed a new plan.

The rest of the day fared no better. Prison food never tasted that great, but for the remainder of the day everything seemed flavoured with ashes. I found it hard to concentrate on anything. In association I even lost a game of chess. Everyone watched me, although that was fairly normal in here.

At lights out I was left alone in the darkness with my fresh concerns, and sleep took a long time coming.

Chapter 14
Death cult

Within a year the inheritance money ran dry, so I turned to dealing for some income. Not the hard stuff — well, not at first. I started with coke and smoke. I did pride myself in selling the finest quality, which made me popular. My abilities meant that I usually avoided most of the problems dealers encountered in that line of work. I always knew if someone wanted to rip me off or screw me over in some way. It also meant I could set things right when they tried.

I had the odd encounter with the police, but my ability enabled me to know whether a quick bribe would do the job, or if I needed to use another form of persuasion. The same went with other potential enemies. I remember one person attempting to rob me. He left screaming without a mark on him and more importantly without any cash or drugs. Word soon spread and no-one bothered me after that. It helped that I was very popular. People always departed happy. Not only did I sell quality product, for those that stayed and chilled for a while would leave feeling better than they did anywhere else.

I remember it as a good time. In contrast to my childhood I discovered that I quite enjoyed being the centre of attention. Regularly dealing with more people helped my powers develop. They increased not just in strength, which made it easier to enter even the most stubborn mind, but also in refinement. The subtleties of manipulating people's highs proved to be an excellent method for mastering thoughts and memories.

Life was good. I spent most of my time stoned and actually managed to bury the hurt so deep inside that it rarely surfaced. On the few occasions that it did, I found that I could now use my own tricks on myself.

My home always entertained a good crowd, all eager to share in my company. That meant women as well, a constant flow of new partners all of whom desired the special touch that only I provided. I've heard it said that a woman's orgasm is emotional as well as physical. My ability more than helped with that. I caught an infection from one of them which proved a little painful as well as a little embarrassing, so I learned to be a bit more cautious. Fame — even of the underground sort — always attracted some attention, but nothing that I couldn't handle.

Acid heralded the end of this easy, carefree life. LSD has quite a reputation and deservedly so. That first trip induced a life changing experience for me. Apparently this happens to many people: they experience new ways of seeing the world or themselves and that can change you. More importantly for me, I discovered new ways of manipulating things. I learned more about the connections between people's thoughts and emotions and the engine that drives them. I could interact at this lower level and gained greater control.

This enhanced control allowed me to create changes in the physical being of the person. I could make their heart beat faster. I could slow it right down. With only a thought I could trigger and rush, as well as modulate its flow.

I started taking acid more regularly and if at first I was clumsy and took the trip into places that people didn't enjoy, it didn't matter. My high now came from more than the drug, it came from the effect I had on those around me. With each trip I refined my technique. From some of the early mistakes I discovered a new thrill. It gave me a greater rush than any I had experienced thus far.

I found that I could take people to the very brink of death. Together we journeyed to the edge and together we stared down into the abyss. This darker tone to the trips scared many of the group away. But some stayed, willing travellers on this morbid journey. New people joined the group, replacing those of faint hearts. They gravitated by word of mouth to this new experience.

Gradually the new group coalesced and stabilised, the more we tripped together, the more in tune we became. After a few months I mastered the ability to take the whole group on the same journey together. I manipulated them all to the very horizon of life so we could gaze into the infinite depths beyond.

Of course, you can't flirt with death without paying a price. One day the inevitable happened. A sweet young Goth girl, desperately in love with death, joined the circle. At a glance I knew exactly what she wanted and we took her where she had never ventured before.

Incidentally it seems a common thing with the young, this fascination with death, but the reality is far more than they ever imagine.

I sank her deep: a sudden plunge to where her life faded. I held her hand as we stood on that shadowed cliff and together we gazed down. In the distance we saw vague shapes moving in the darkness. On previous journeys I had tried to reach them, to bring them to my grasp, but they were elusive and always remained just out of reach. It was odd, but people who had made the same trip on their own never saw these forms. They only appeared if I was present.

There is a definite boundary between life and death. We always travelled right up to it, but never beyond. Even I felt wary of crossing that veil. There I stood with this pretty girl, and we both looked down. I remember her name was Melissa. I brought in the rest of group, seven of us in total, and together we stood transfixed by the terrible wonder of it.

Without any warning she jumped off the cliff and plummeted, dragging me in her wake.

In that moment I knew panic. As I fell so did the others. The shapes below us become agitated, frenzied in sudden excitement. I now sensed their hunger that somehow had been hidden from me before. One part of me, immune from that panic, noticed that no matter how far we fell, they appeared to get no closer.

I wrestled with the fear and conquered it. I pulled back, seeking to arrest the fall and rise again. Melissa's eagerness to embrace that which lurked below dragged me further into the abyss. Bound to me, the others screamed their descent.

With an effort like none I had ever managed before I wrenched myself free from her clutches and slowed my fall. The pain from the effort shrieked throughout my form. I ignored it, watching her continue to fall, quickly vanishing from sight. With another agonizing surge I managed to start rising, but the weight of the others prevented me. Again I pulled, but a couple of the other minds slipped from my grasp.

Looking back, I wonder — did I let them go intentionally?

The lessened weight freed me and in an instant I returned to the world, released from Melissa's fading mind. Struggling for breath I first checked her, and then the other bodies. Three of them lay still. They were dead, their faces drawn in shock. Besides myself, three others survived but they panicked and ran before I could react, leaving me alone.

Word of what had happened would soon spread. If I reacted quicker I could have convinced the others to remain silent, to cover up what had occurred. I did not, so now I had to do this alone. The house where we lived was old; there was no physical damage to the corpses, so I started an electrical fire, and waited for the flames to take hold before making my own escape.

Chapter 15
Final day in court

I woke on the Monday morning still unsettled from the previous day's events. This new priest worried me. He might only be one man, but coupled with Hammond's own apparent immunity this presented a risk I couldn't afford. I decided to change my plan. Hammond would need to be dealt with immediately. That very day in fact. I'd lose a few prisoners to the block or the hospital wing, but getting Hammond out of the way for good would be worth that loss.

I pondered on the best approach. I required enough prisoners to make the attack overwhelming. I couldn't allow any possibility of failure. That meant it had to happen either at meal time or during association. Association would be the best time to do it. I'd distract the other guards while some of my implanted prisoners did the deed. Doing it in association also meant that my dinner would not be disturbed.

As for the Friar, without Hammond to save him and with all the other guards and prisoners already subsumed I would deal with him easily. Nothing fancy: I had no idea how he blocked my talent, but it wouldn't stop a blade. With the prison takeover starting from the chapel on Sunday morning he would be right in the thick of it, and if he offered any trouble then I'd kill him quickly. Otherwise we could take our time with him. He'd also make an ideal hostage, someone to show off when the cameras arrived.

Those thoughts cheered me up enough to actually enjoy breakfast, including the lumpy porridge. While being processed for transportation I considered the day ahead. The time had come to step things up a notch. I'd sabotaged the witnesses already. Next I would play with the judge and jury. I'd always planned to leave the judge until last and I saw no reason to change that, so for today it would be the jurors. I'd have a bit of fun and then be sent back down to the cells.

I wondered how long they'd keep going if a juror died each day?

I was definitely in a better mood by the time we arrived at the courthouse. Even the weather had cleared up, allowing some winter sunshine into the cubicle. One of the officers even provided me with an old newspaper and a cup of tea while I waited to be summoned. Time dragged by, and the poor night's sleep didn't help. I felt a little drowsy when the cell door finally opened. The two guards walked me up the familiar stairs into the courtroom.

Immediately I realised that something wasn't right.

I scanned the court and it was empty. No jurors waited for the proceedings to begin. In front of me no lawyers or their assistants at the bench. I looked behind me, the public gallery bereft of reporters.

Suddenly I felt nauseous.

The only people in the room were the two guards flanking me and the two police officers standing at the door.

A wave of drowsiness almost dropped me to my knees.

The tea! They'd put something in my tea.

I surged inside myself, manipulated microscopic triggers within my own brain. I desperately sought anything to counter the tiredness that threatened to overwhelm me.

The judge entered the room — a different one from before. The door between the policemen opened and more officers marched into the room. I continued forcing my mind to ignore the siren call of whatever they had put in my drink. I felt my balance slipping.

The judge spoke, his voice echoing from a great distance. I couldn't concentrate. "This trial is concluded," he told me. "A mistrial has been declared. We have released the jurors from their service."

I heard the words, but struggled to comprehend their meaning. Strong hands gripped my arms. I split my concentration and cast my mind at the judge. Apparently he knew the same trick as the Friar, because I rebounded off him. With a sinking feeling I tried again. I bounced off the sheer surface of his mind.

Finally I managed some success against the drug in my veins, and my mind cleared a little. The judge continued speaking.

"Evidence in a secret session concerning your association with known terrorists has come to light. You are now being detained under the Prevention of Terrorism Act. An application for your extradition has already been submitted and approved under emergency powers."

I hadn't anticipated this. Not this quickly.

The police moved in. The guards took a firmer hold, but with an effort I broke free from their grip. I jabbed to one side, striking a glancing blow to the first guard's neck. I spun round and nearly fell. Simultaneously I lashed out with my mind as well. This one raised no defence against me. He didn't even have time to cry out before he collapsed in a trembling heap to the floor.

The fog still clouded my thinking. I stomped on the other guard as he attempted to rise, and cast my mind towards the policeman charging towards me. Within those few seconds I found myself crowded. I fought on anyway, smashed my mind into the heads of the uniforms around me. Two of them staggered, clutching their heads. The others kept coming. I blocked the baton strike of one and then staggered myself. A burning sensation flared in my side.

Another tazer discharged into my ribs and I fell, the electricity forced me to dance. A baton struck hard against my neck as another burn blossomed. A scuffed boot was the last thing I saw.

Chapter 16
A bloody business

Unfortunately the house fire didn't cover my tracks as well as I'd hoped. The problem wasn't the police — their investigation ceased as soon as the fire brigade confirmed the cause as accidental. The bodies were identified as three known drug users and teenage delinquents, so the deaths soon faded from the public eye.

Melissa's family proved a different matter. The Jacobs were well known throughout the area. Where people wouldn't talk to the police, they would talk to the family, if they knew what was good for them. She might have been one of many distant cousins in the family, but that wasn't important. Harm against one was a slight against all. The word on the street identified me as the killer.

I know; I was very careless. A bit of thought and I could have avoided a lot of trouble.

The first I learned of this was my front door being kicked in. I'd lain low for a while, keeping my head down until the police interest died back. The group kept away, but the need to keep my personal stash stocked meant meeting a few people. I stopped taking acid. It wasn't the same on my own and that particular drug now posed a danger to me. I tripped alone a few times, but found it all too easy to become lost in myself. I delved deeper and deeper until there was no me at all, just the barest of impulses. Eventually I would return to my senses, hours later and without a clue where the time had disappeared to. I became afraid of this killing emptiness that stole these pieces away from me.

From then on I stuck to the smoke and a little coke as a pick me up now and then. A few joints put me into a mellow mood and I was sitting just staring at the TV when the door crashed in. Three generations of the Jacobs stood before me — and they looked pissed. It put a dampener on my mood, I can tell you. I jumped up as they charged in. Glimpsing into their minds, all I sensed was the murder they planned.

Being stoned, my reflexes weren't what they normally would be. I threw the first punch, but the girl's brother caught the wild swing and returned a better aimed blow of his own. It clipped my jaw and I stumbled back. Before I regained my balance the other two seized my arms. The brother kept coming and punched me hard in the stomach. The blow doubled me over. The other two immediately pulled me back upright, and desperately I gasped for breath. I lashed out with my mind, but the pain disturbed my concentration and I failed to gain a hold.

Another blow hammered into my stomach before the attacker stepped back and pulled a knife from his jacket. With a sneer he told me why I was about to die. I had killed his sister and now it was my turn.

That was his mistake.

In that short gap I regained my breath and summoned my will and, with clearer focus, unleashed it upon him. I smashed into his mind and blinded him. In response he lunged forwards and slashed wildly with the blade. I twisted his spatial perception so he swung high. I ducked easily under the blade and the knife slashed across the faces of the two men holding me. Both cried out and released me.

The brother swung the blade a second time. Again he missed me and further injured his compatriots. I kicked him savagely in the knee cap, which cracked as he fell. I snatched up the fallen knife and turned to the other two men. I leapt forwards and stabbed the older man in the stomach. He grunted and collapsed, taking the knife with him.

The other now seemed more interested in his bleeding wounds than me. A single punch to the side of the neck knocked him to the floor. It's better to be safe than sorry, so I retrieved the knife and thrust it into his throat. Covered in his blood I fled from the house.

Outside in a parked car another man watched me leave. He started to climb out of car. Before he could get out I threw myself against the door, stunning him for a vital moment. Before he recovered I dragged him from the car, then slammed the door against his skull. I hit him a second time and after the third let him collapse to the ground. I kicked him in the head to make sure and climbed in the car.

I never learned how to drive. On TV it looked pretty simple. Unfortunately, it wasn't so simple and I stalled the car a few yards down the road. I got out and ran. I ran to the only person I could think of who would help me. I ran to Psycho Steve.

No-one called him Psycho Steve to his face, not more than once anyway. I didn't know him well. We were nodding acquaintances at best, but no-one messed with him, not even the Jacobs family and that made his house a safe haven.

He didn't seem surprised to see me, although he never seemed surprised by anything. From his reputation you would have expected to see a huge beast of a man. The reality was that he was small, quiet, and capable of incredible ultra-violence in the blink of an eye. He radiated such ferocity that even I baulked at entering his mind. He invited me in while asking whether I knew that "the whole fucking town was looking for me?"

I did now, but I hadn't yet decided what I would do about it. I had few choices. The first was to stay and battle it out, but even Steve thought that was a bad idea. "They'll keep coming," he told me, especially now more of them had been hurt. I could hand myself into the police, but Steve would gut me himself if I did that and I wouldn't be safe there anyway. They'd lock me up — and trapped in prison I'd be an easier target than I already was.

Hiding in the town wasn't an option either. They'd find me sooner or later, so that left running. I would have to leave town. "Just get yourself far gone and fucking disappear," Steve eloquently advised. And good advice it was too. I'd be safe there for the night and I could crash on the couch and rest up. He rolled a fat one and we chilled for a while listening to some tunes on the stereo.

Before lunch the next day Steve drove me to the train station. He didn't want to know where I was going, just repeated his advice to get myself well gone. I decided to head north and paid for my ticket, but the platform looked too open and exposed, so I decided to wait out of view in the station bar.

That was my mistake.

The train was due in less than an hour. As usual the timetable couldn't be relied upon. I sat in a corner, out of view. With the clear vision of hindsight it's obvious that I should have kept a watchful eye on the barman, but I didn't, so I didn't know that he recognized me and telephoned one of the Jacobs he was friendly with, eager to curry favour.

After half an hour nursing a fruit juice, I heard the station announcer inform everyone that the train would be delayed by fifteen minutes. Annoying, but no big deal — all par the course for travelling with British Rail. The door to the bar opened and a crowd of the Jacobs and their cronies walked in. The barman made himself scarce, leaving me alone with them. This was not going to end well.

My only advantage was they appeared in no hurry. I had nowhere to run and they outnumbered me. They saw me as easy prey.

That was their mistake.

I stood and pushed the table over in front of me. It wasn't much of a barrier but it would slow them down a little. I flung my glass at the leader and unleashed the fury from my mind. I took the mind of one and savaged it with my will. He collapsed screaming, and his friends stumbled over his twitching form.

A distorted voice from the tannoy announced that my train would soon be arriving from platform three.

I picked up the stool I'd been sitting on and threw it as I simultaneously torpedoed into the mind of another. He screamed before slumping to the floor weeping, his mind shredded. Now I could hear the train arriving.

The others slowed their approach as they comprehended the wrongness of the situation around them. Here was my chance. Although my head ached from the bursts of power I had used, I cast out again, causing a wave of dizziness to wash over my attackers. It slowed them a little more. With the sound of opening train doors I charged the leader. A flutter of surprise crossed his face as I ran at him. He was big, too big to charge through, so I let myself bounce round him and sped for the door.

The quicker ones tried to grab me, but they lacked bulk and I charged through, crashing through the doors. The few passengers stared in shock at the sudden violent scene. The platform guard's whistle blew as I raced towards the train. As the doors closed I jumped onboard with only the muffled, empty curses behind me.

Chapter 17
A bad wake up

Every part of me ached when I regained consciousness. They must have done quite a number on me while I was out. I felt an impressive collection of bruising all over my body. The burns on my ribs where they had zapped me added a treble pain to the bass of the beating.

It took some effort to open my eyes, and to be honest I didn't really want to. Things felt bad enough already. I didn't need special abilities to know I was in a tight spot. To my surprise, when I did finally brave opening my eyes I saw nothing at all, only darkness. No light illuminated wherever I now lay; only the cold, hard floor below me provided any sensation. I wondered how long I had been out. My head still felt clouded from the drug they slipped me, so I guessed that it must have only been a few hours.

I tried to move, but couldn't. My arms were bound tight across my chest, each hand secured against the opposite shoulder. The only movement I managed was a worm-like thrash that succeeded only in banging my head against the floor. A new pain added to the collection.

To add to my indignity I realised that I was naked. Only the itchy bindings on my arms and legs provided any form of covering. The comforting warmth of unconsciousness soon faded, leaving me cold.

I still couldn't concentrate. I struggled against the leaden cloud to focus. I fought to summon my will, but it remained just out of reach. A great confusion fogged my mind. I surrendered to it and let sleep engulf me.

I did not dream.

Some unknown time later I awoke. This time as I opened my eyes harsh white light blinded me — so bright it lanced into my skull. I quickly closed my eyes again. Keeping them firmly shut I allowed a groan to escape and felt the pain fade slightly. A pang of nausea swept through my gut. When it passed I gingerly opened my eyes again. Gradually they adjusted and with my constricted movement I tried to look around.

It was obvious I lay in a different cell, but in many ways it might as well be the same one — four walls, ceiling and floor — a concrete box around me. I noticed some differences, the first being the lack of windows. There was no furniture either. Layers of paint made the floor beneath me smooth, but still uncomfortable. Its chill against my back drained what little warmth I had from my skin. I saw the outline of a door, painted the same ochre colour as the walls. A light bulb covered in fine mesh bathed me in its glow.

The period of sleep had dulled the aches, but my body was still sore.

I twisted my head and could now see that I was bound in a straightjacket. They hadn't gagged me so I was able to shout out, and I yelled until my voice cracked hoarse. I heard no response. My own voice echoed back at me.

I blamed the lingering effects of the drugs in my system for not realising sooner. It took more than walls to imprison me, but I found it more difficult than usual to release my will. Again I blamed the drugs. I calmed myself and tried again. It took a few attempts before I finally escaped the confines of my body.

It felt good to be free from my bindings. Eagerly I attempted to pass through the adjacent wall. My mind hit a barrier and passed no further. Thinking back I shouldn't have been surprised, but I was. I tried again, frantically this time, but could not penetrate the wall.

I gathered all my weakened strength to try again. The effort met the same result. My will splashed against the surface, a feeble wave against its solidity. I probed the other walls, searched for a weak spot — even a small chink would do. Nothing. I started to panic. I probed the floor, the door and the ceiling. Near the light I detected a gap, but when I squeezed my will through I encountered a new barrier.

Exhausted, I gave up. My head pounded and my stomach growled. How long had it been since I last ate? My mouth remained dry, I needed a drink. I worked my tongue, tried to create some saliva. At the thought of a cool glass of water I struggled angrily against the straitjacket, twisted and pulled with my arms.

Drained, I eventually admitted defeat and let sleep claim me again.

Some unknown time later I awoke. I followed the same routine, burned more energy to no avail. My stomach felt increasingly hollow, the hunger another pain for my growing collection. My mouth parched. I felt increasing pressure in my bladder.

I was trapped and could not escape.

Chapter 18
A new beginning

I disappeared north. Apart from the odd day trip and infrequent holidays with my mother I'd never been outside of Lewes. It felt strange, like I had lost some part of myself that I could never get back. The carnage back at the train station would merit a proper investigation from the police. I had never been in trouble with the law so they didn't have my fingerprints. All they would have is a name and a face. Both were easily changed.

The Jacobs wouldn't give up looking either, but here I was less concerned. They were big fish in a small pond. If I didn't attract the wrong sort of attention I would never see them again.

As for me, I had no real plan. I did know one thing: from then I would remain out of sight — but not out of mind.

After travelling through London I left the train and walked. I walked north for several weeks. I thought of nothing, just placed one foot ahead of the other. I focused only on moving forward. I found it invigorating. I drifted unseen through a world I didn't know. In some ways it calmed my mind, although it didn't answer the question of what I would do next.

I finally stopped when I encountered a grey, dismal city. Here in this concrete jungle I could lose myself. For days I walked the streets, learning the terrain. This seemed to be a place of contrasts. At the centre was a small, thriving financial district surrounded by a bustling commercial area. On the outskirts and along the filthy river, abandoned factories lay rusting and empty. Some had been replaced with stylish if expensive flats for the up-and-comers. These were in the minority: most of the city formed from small pockets of fortified shops, surrounded by rough, decaying estates filled with the poor and hopeless.

It wasn't just the place that contrasted. The people were the same: some full of hope and eager for the future, while others wallowed in their misery, wishing for the past.

Even in my bedraggled state I could have used my talent to lodge in a hotel, or somebody's home. Instead I picked a different path. I chose to sleep rough. Initially it provided a way to keep unnoticed. I soon learned that the anonymity comforted me. It made me feel safe. Each night I sought out a new quiet spot where I could sleep undisturbed.

Two months passed and I felt myself becoming ever more isolated. I allowed myself to grow further removed from the press of humanity. I thought that no bad thing. I had already made the mistake of mixing with other people and it hadn't ended well, so for now I would remain apart. The money Steve gave me didn't last long. A patchy beard now covered my face. I rarely washed and when I did it was in public lavatories. I smelled awful. I sensed the revulsion of people that passed me by and it amused me.

Eventually I became bored. That has always been my weakness. To amuse myself I invented a game to pass the time. I secured a spot near the train station where the trains unloaded the swarm of commuters each morning. I watched them as they walked by. I never begged: when I felt hungry I picked a passer-by and they handed me their money. They then walked away, confused by their sudden act of charity.

Every day I observed this surge of humanity sweep past me, a tide that passed first one way and then the other at the end of the day. I immersed myself in their minds, diving in their thoughts. I felt powerful to gain such understanding of these people. These daily migrations to the beast of commerce provided the highlights of my day, the beat by which I measured the passing of time.

At first I contented myself to watch them, to glimpse the fragments of their lives and to help myself to whatever I needed to sustain me. Eventually, though, I became bored and I began to judge them.

Twice a day I lost myself in this swarm of petty misery and even pettier dreams. I picked lives at random and followed the threads. These people didn't know that I felt what they felt, that I observed the secrets that haunted them. To begin with I judged them by their own standards, or at least by the standards of the world around them.

That restraint lasted for almost a month. Bored again, I started to condemn them.

The first victim was a banker. I never bothered to learn their names. This banker liked to beat his wife with his fists, but he never found the courage to stand up to his boss. He could never explain why he strolled into the wrong part of town. Wearing his expensive suit he stood out and threatened the youths hanging around a local shop when they mocked him. They must have been surprised when he kept thanking them as they hit him, but that didn't stop them beating him until he could thank them no more.

I settled into a routine, one every morning and one every evening. Two people every day, their privacy invaded and their successes or failures judged.

There was a woman who cheated on her husband and then blamed him for the breakup of their marriage. She was making her way to her lawyer, anticipating a generous divorce. After walking by she stripped herself naked in the street and offered herself to every man who passed by. One man even accepted the offer, although he soon regretted the decision when the police arrived.

Day in, day out I picked two more. Not only did I enjoy these brief interludes, I derived a certain satisfaction in devising suitable punishments for their crimes.

Another was the father who liked to touch his daughter. After work he walked to the nearest school, stripped down and shouted for them to send out the whores. He could barely touch himself, let alone others by the time he reached the police cell.

Before too long it stopped being judgement — it didn't matter what they had done, it became a sport. A sport with only one rule, two people a day must play. All I needed was some spark from which I could draw more suffering.

One afternoon a man who had been attracted to his co-worker for years, but never raised the courage to invite her for coffee, tried to rape her as soon as he saw her at work the next morning.

For many months I did this. I didn't speak to anyone, just trawled through their minds. Like some beast of the deep, I sifted for thoughts or emotions to inspire me. And for their part, they just walked on by. Those who were close enough would turn their nose at the stench of me. They saw only another dirty homeless bum to be avoided, but they couldn't avoid me.

At night I would find somewhere out of the way to sleep, somewhere quiet where I could rest undisturbed. My sleep back then was always dreamless, the sweet oblivion that I yearned for. After some months passed I started to hate the moment I would awake. When I slept I felt nothing, saw nothing. When I was awake the constant buzz of humanity infected my every moment.

Twice a day I struck back and two people paid the price.

One night I didn't find a safe enough shelter for the night and a gang of drunken youths looking for easy sport woke me. For the first time in months I spoke to another human being, physically interacted with them. It felt good to let it all out.

A woman walking to the shops discovered their bodies the next morning. For a few weeks the city filled with a hue and cry, but as always no-one saw the filthy tramp at the edge of their vision. They just walked on by.

Chapter 19
In limbo

I lost count of the number of times I woke in that cell. On the fourth occasion I came to in a pool of my own urine. I tried to shuffle out of the stinking puddle, but I only smeared it over more of my body. So there I lay, caked in my own crusted filth, the smell of my own piss and shit assaulting my nostrils. Breathing through my mouth helped a little.

The light was always on, an angry eye glaring down at me. It never stopped watching me. I wondered who hid behind that eye. Were they watching me now? What did they want?

Still I hadn't received any food or water. My mouth was now so dry it pained me to breathe. My stomach cramped, sending waves of nausea through my body. To compound this I started seeing things. At first it was just little things, crawlies at the edge of my vision. As time passed they grew. Something lurked behind me — I heard it slithering. I tried to see this hidden menace, but I couldn't.

At the edge of my hearing faint whispers tormented me. With fading strength and building rage I expanded my awareness and the presence fled, leaving me alone.

The hallucinations didn't trouble me at first. Everyone who takes drugs for a long period of time, especially psychedelics, will experience them sooner or later. This was different. I wasn't on a high. This was the thirst that clawed at my throat, the hunger that gnawed in my guts. At times it felt so bad my control slipped and I moaned and cried out.

I never received a reply.

Again and again I tried to escape, to free my mind from the confines of this cell. I found no weakness and each attempt drained me that little bit more. I probed the gap around the light, but it was just a tease. I could touch the gap, fiddle with it even, but full penetration eluded me.

Seeking a different refuge I recalled the trips I experienced a lifetime ago. In them I delved deep within my own mind, travelled the inner landscape. This brought small relief, and helped fill the time. I couldn't free myself from the discomfort caused by hunger and thirst for long. I could only descend so far, then physical need always dragged me back.

I thought back to the abyss: there was a freedom they couldn't deny me. For a while I contemplated this. I won't deny it wasn't tempting. It would at least release me from this suffering. Doubt and pride prevented me.

The doubt came from not knowing what happens next. I've never been a religious person, so I did not know what happens after the moment of death. These days it's fashionable to claim that nothing exists, that the physical is all we are. When you die, that is it. If that were true, then I would have been all for it — welcomed it with open arms, even. Sweet oblivion had a nice lure to it.

Of course I know better now.

Alone in my misery I worried. What if the atheists were wrong? What if death wasn't simply the end, but the beginning of something new, as many believed? If that was true, what guarantee that it would be better than where I was now?

This led to another concern.

I was well aware that I possessed an unusual ability, and until recently I hadn't encountered anybody who could deliberately obstruct my power. And while it was certainly true that I was at a disadvantage, that wouldn't always be the case. If my captors did end up killing me then it would make no difference anyway.

But I had come here — well not here precisely, but the whole point of allowing myself to be arrested in the first place, was to die. Suicide by cop, writ large. Did it matter that my plan failed, that I wouldn't be the terrible legend I had set out to be?

In the grand scheme of things it probably didn't matter. It did matter to me though. I wanted everyone to know what I had done. Not only that, but to worry what I could have done. One day there will be another like me and I wanted everyone to fear that day as that new version of me arises and sees my example and strives to be far worse.

A satisfying thought.

So why did I not aim higher? Instead of a grand stand costing hundreds of lives I could have committed more, far more. I could have brought hell itself to the world, or at least a pretty close facsimile. Why didn't I? It's not like I was squeamish or anything.

I know there are other questions that I avoided. I found myself drifting through my past. I examined my deeds, explored how things could have been different.

I returned to the real question: what did the people on the other side of that door want? Was this just punishment? A means to make me suffer? Could it be something more? Did they want something from me?

Now there was an interesting thought.

So I lay there, stinking of my own bodily waste and thought of my doom and I smiled. I realised I had done what I had because I needed to, because I wanted to. If I was to die here then so be it, but if that door opened, I would not beg.

So I waited.

Chapter 20
Time for a last stand

My second winter on the streets started drawing in. The previous winter had been bitter, but this one promised to be far worse. This would be a winter that thinned the numbers of homeless from the streets. A blessing for many no doubt. I weathered the previous winter, but this one I wasn't so sure. I didn't even know if I wanted to.

Over the past two years I had changed. The most apparent change was physical. I aged considerably. When I glanced upon my reflection in the glass of the shop fronts I no longer saw a young man in his early twenties. I appeared much older. The seasons weathered my skin. A long, ragged beard obscured my face, and my hair now hung longer, a matted mess across my shoulders.

I changed inside as well. I still maintained the twice daily routine, trawling through the thousands of minds that passed me by each day. One every morning and one every evening, two people every day tormented by my whim.

It passed the time and provided some focus to the day, this infecting people's lives. I no longer worried too much about the judgement. Their failures didn't really matter. The effect I had kept me going, although I have to confess that it no longer provided the thrill that it once did. It became a habit rather than a cause.

One of the few things beyond my power forced me to make a choice. If I continued as things were, I might survive the winter, or I might not. I could have secured warmer accommodation and continued the daily routine — that was the easy option. Or I could have done something completely different, travelled maybe.

For a time I pondered these choices and eventually came to a conclusion. There was nothing I wanted to do. What I did each day no longer provided me with any satisfaction. The thought of something else didn't appeal either. To coin a phrase, I lacked life goals.

That caused me to consider my legacy. Essentially I had none. I had become the ultimate grey man. No-one knew who I was. No-one knew of my activities. If I died now, no-one would ever know anything. I would only be another statistic. That bothered me more than not having a future. I had brought great ruination to many and the world would never know. That hardly seemed fair. It wasn't fair on my victims, the public, or to me.

I remember smiling as the plan began to form. I should be judged. I should be judged for what I was and for what I had done. Yes, and in their judgement I would create a mini apocalypse at the heart of the safety they held dear. Take away the laws, and the courts and the prisons that protected them. I would take away their faith in the system.

I imagined a glorious last stand and I would claim my legacy. First I needed to get arrested — and I also wanted an audience.

Once decided on my course of action, I wasted no time. I stood up and freed myself from the pile of dirty blankets that swaddled me. The nearest person was an old lady, walking unsteadily to the shops. Today she walked to collect her pension. She would never need to collect her pittance again. I snatched the cane that supported her and struck her across the face. She collapsed without a sound. The crowd around me panicked like sheep — some rushed away, averting their eyes, while others froze in shock.

Only two from the crowd made any move towards me. The first was an old man, whose pride in past glories drove him forwards. The other was a younger man. His youthful immortality filled him with bravado. The old man was nearer, so I took him down first, using the old woman's cane to batter him to the ground. The cane broke as I hammered it down one last time into his skull. I drove the broken remnant into the stomach of the young guy as he charged in.

More people fled as the youth clutched his stomach, squealing in a most undignified fashion. His feeling of immortality vanished in that moment. A dead zone formed around me. People feared to cross into this dread circle.

I stood, waited for the first police to arrive. They arrived quickly, well within the expected response time. The young man no longer screamed, although he still clutched his stomach. He only managed a low moan. It sounded like this faithless boy was praying.

The two officers climbed out of their patrol car and approached cautiously. They didn't want to come any closer. They'd rather wait for reinforcements, but that didn't suit my plans at all: I wanted a spectacle that all here would remember and something juicy enough for those watching the news later on to enjoy.

I resisted a temptation to urinate on the old woman's face, although that would shock them into moving, it would also leave me at a disadvantage. So I kicked the wounded youth instead, forcing a louder cry from him.

The two officers still hesitated, but they outnumbered me and I appeared unarmed so they moved in. They held their batons tight as they approached, diverging so I had to split my attention. Normally that would be a good tactic; unfortunately it wouldn't help them this time. The one on my blind side felt my mind smash through his like a freight train.

The other paused as he saw his partner collapse for no apparent reason. This allowed me time to close the distance. He swung the baton, striking a glancing blow on my arm. The many thin layers of clothing absorbed the blow. I kicked his legs from beneath him. He swung a desperate strike as he fell and another as my hands closed around his throat.

Naturally, he struggled. He was young and strong and almost managed to throw me off. I focused my will on his motor control centres; he lost the strength in his arms then his body. Then he really panicked. Only I felt his desperate struggles, now only feeble twitches as I crushed the life from him.

I still strangled him long after he died. The armed response team arrived. Now I would have to be careful. As I'd hoped, a large crowd gathered to watch unfolding events. Some held mobile phones pointed in my direction — even better. The armed officers piled out of their van, guns at the ready. I let the dead officer fall to the road and stepped away with my hands held high.

The armed response team saw their dead and disabled colleagues and their trigger fingers tightened. Their training held their fire. I sensed their desire for me to make the wrong move. I calculated that I could probably take down some of them before the bullets hit, but could I take them all quickly enough? I thought not, and besides, I wanted to get captured. Phase one now completed, I had to survive long enough to enter a courtroom.

Carefully I stepped away from the bodies, my hands still held high, open and empty. I turned slowly and obeyed their shouted commands. Within moments I lay face down on the ground, a knee pressed painfully into my back. They handcuffed me, then dragged me into the waiting police van.

During the journey to the police station I received more than a few punches and kicks. It was only to be expected and the sergeant in command of the team prevented it from getting too serious. I took the blows without comment. Now was the time for keeping silent.

At the police station they tried to process me. I refused to provide my name or any details about myself. I refused to make any comment when they tried to question me, and I declined legal representation. The only answer I provided was "Now is not the time."

After twelve hours they brought me a meal, burger and chips from a local takeaway. Outside the door I heard them spit on it, so it I left it uneaten. Shortly afterwards a doctor visited and checked my injuries: a few cuts and many bruises, but nothing for him to worry about. With the formalities out of the way they charged me with five counts of murder, along with sundry other charges before they presented me before a magistrate and she remanded me in prison for trial.

Chapter 21
The opening shots

    The door finally opened. I couldn't even guess how long I'd lain there. I'd lost count of the number of times I had slept and woken in this cell. The stench was overwhelming and when the door suddenly opened it released just enough fresh air to provide some relief. I turned as best I could to face the open door, to see who had entered.
    I noticed a strange thing. While my hunger pains seemed to have abated somewhat, I felt a new sharp pain in one of my arms. At the time I didn't think much of it. I assumed it to be some side effect of being starved and thirsty for so long. Looking back, I must have been subjected to extended psychological torture. They kept me drugged and starved to weaken my will. Only from my new perspective did I piece this together, but back then I didn't have a clue.
    The Friar walked in, his black robes a stark contrast with the pallid walls. I fixated on the cross, with its necklace of beads dangling from his neck. He carried a plastic cup with a clear straw in one hand. He watched me closely as he entered, stepping with exaggerated care around the puddle of piss. I knew it was a wasted effort, but I still struggled weakly against my bonds to reach this bastard. I balled up what little strength I possessed and threw at him. Like the first time I met him, my will

bounced off. I attempted to grip his mind, to crush through his defence.

The Friar revealed no hint of my assault. He crouched beside me, perfectly calm, the venom in my stare of no concern to him. He stared at me for a few seconds then told me that he was Friar Francis Magnus.

I know, motherfucker. I remember.

He told me that he was ordained as a member of the Dominican order. That fact wasn't important then — it became relevant later. For now he represented whoever had me locked up in this toilet. As a member of the order, he worked with the Vatican, specifically alongside the Holy Inquisition. For a long time the Vatican held secret agreements with most governments for the handling of special prisoners.

Now that was interesting.

Special prisoners that the regular authorities couldn't handle. I had been extradited from the UK and I would never see the outside world again. He paused for a moment then said, unless I co-operated.

Another interesting thought. So they did want something.

He offered me the cup of water, I nodded and he placed the straw to my lips. I drank deeply. The cool water tasted delicious as it trickled down my throat. I suppressed the urge to spit it in his face.

The Friar smiled that odd little smile of his as if congratulating me on my restraint. That infuriated me and I succumbed to the urge. Stupid I know, but it provided some fleeting satisfaction.

He wiped the water from his face, that smile still in place. "We'll talk again," he told me and then left.

Some time later the door opened again. This time Hammond entered. He wasn't alone. A man dressed in an identical black suit came in with him. If you gave them both hats and they could have been the Blues Brothers. The thought made me smile. The other man held an empty syringe. They wanted to draw blood from me. The struggle to prevent them doing so would be pointless, but I tried anyway. In my weakened state Hammond immobilised me easily, as if restraining a child or invalid. They moved in with the needle — and with a sharp scratch the job was done. Just as quickly as they entered, they left.

Alone once again, I wondered how long they would leave me for this time. At least they had given me something to ponder. Two things in fact. The first was that they needed me for something. The second that there were others like me, others for whom they made special arrangements to contain. Were they in this building? Was there someone like me also lying in their own filth on the other side of the wall?

I let myself sleep.

The sound of the door opening woke me. The Friar again.

I'd waited for this moment. Gently this time I probed his mind, searching for any weakness. I received another one of those odd smiles for my efforts. He let me drink. This time the water tasted sweet, but he didn't say anything and left after I had satisfied my thirst.

He left me alone again. I slept.

This pattern repeated several times, maybe more. By that point I had completely lost track of the passing time. On one occasion, I felt stronger and when Hammond and his assistant returned, I launched a mental assault. As before, entering Hammond's mind was easy — I passed through it like water. His mind was barren, everything of importance locked inside the imposing monolith sat at the centre of his being. I smashed against the rock, this fortress at the core of his soul. I saw a grimace flash across his face. He could feel me! Encouraged, I attacked again, lashing against this obsidian totem that defied me. Hammond gripped me tightly, held me secure for the blood to be drained.

I switched to the assistant, hoping that he would make an easier victim. He cried out as I smashed through the thin veil with which he hoped to protect his mind. Hammond realised my change in approach and reacted quickly. He punched me in the face, knocking me back into the darkness.

The pattern resumed, but I no longer resisted. I shifted to playing the long game. Trussed up I could not capitalise on any mental assault.

More unmeasured time passed.

I think it must have been days before I started feeling stronger, more coherent. I pretended to be a good boy, not resisting as blood was taken from me. I offered only thanks when the Friar brought me the sweet water.

While I felt stronger, the hollowness in my stomach still gnawed at me. They'd provided the sweetened water, but still no food.

This time when I woke, I scanned the cell again. Once again I probed the walls for any weakness. I probed gently, just feeling for anything different. I still found only the same flaw, a small gap by the light in the ceiling. I teased at it, tried to pry at it. There was no give. An idea blossomed and I attempted something different, pouring myself into that narrow space. I squeezed myself in and when I filled the crack I expanded my will.

At first I felt a slight give as something shifted and then suddenly stopped. I exerted myself again, but there was no reaction this time. I withdrew back inside myself and relaxed. Not long later the cell door opened and the Friar walked in. He again let me drink the sweet tasting water from his cup. I didn't attempt to probe his mind.

He looked at me and asked if I was ready to talk. I responded by asking whether it meant getting out of this pool of my own filth. He smiled and assured me that it would. In that case I was more than happy to talk.

He exited the cell but didn't close the door. Hammond then entered. I still couldn't get used to him not wearing the prison officer uniform. He didn't look right in civilian clothes, as if he belonged in a uniform. Without saying a word he unbuckled me from the straightjacket and helped me to my feet.

Hammond led me from the cell. We entered a corridor, which ended with a sturdy steel door. Opposite my cell was another one exactly the same, and beside that another door lay open. Hammond guided me through it. My legs trembled from the exertion, weakened from lying down for so long.

With some delight, I discovered a shower and toilet inside. The spray from the shower felt warm and wonderful. I luxuriated in the cascading water, soaped myself and let the water sluice the crust from my body. My escort stood by the door, kept me in his peripheral vision, but allowed me a modicum of privacy.

I left the water running long after my skin felt clean, just enjoying its touch. I was tempted to peek into Hammond's mind to see what would happen next. I resisted that temptation. I assumed that my behaviour was being monitored in some way and now was not the time.

Finally feeling more human than I had for some time I exited the shower. Hammond passed me a large towel. My stomach growled indignantly as I dried myself. I hoped that some food would be in my near future. Hammond took the towel from me and then passed me some clothing to wear. The clothes were like linen pyjamas, loose and light on my skin. It felt pleasant to wear some clothes that didn't restrain me. He then gave me slippers for my feet and led me to the room next door.

The room looked very similar to my cell, painted the same colour, but it didn't smell of my bodily waste. I considered that a plus. In the centre of the room stood a small table with two chairs, each placed opposite the other. I noticed that the items of furniture were bolted to the floor. On the table waited a bowl of soup and a plastic cup of fruit juice.

Hammond took position by the door as I tucked into the welcome food and drink. They both tasted great and I ate leisurely, taking my time to savour the flavours. As I finished the last drops of soup Friar Francis walked in and while Hammond cleared away the bowl and cup, he sat down and said:

"Let's talk."

Chapter 22
The first chat

We looked at each other across the table. He opened by telling me what I already knew.

"As I'm sure you remember my name is Friar Francis Magnus. I am a member of the Dominican Order."

Like a gentleman of old, he offered his hand to me. I hesitated for a moment, suspecting a trap. After an uncomfortable pause I shook his hand. His grip was firmer than expected but not overbearing. It occurred to me that I didn't know the significance of his order.

"The Dominican Order? I don't understand what that means."

"Some call us the Black Friars." He indicated the black habit he wore. "We were formed many centuries ago, to preach the Gospel and to combat heresy."

Heresy: the word sounded familiar, a legacy from a church educated youth. I couldn't recall its meaning, so again I asked for clarification.

As a member of the order of preachers he was eager to teach. "Heresy is the corruption of the teachings of the church," he explained.

"Is that really an issue in this day and age?" I couldn't help but smile. And as some fragment of a news story bubbled to the surface, I asked, "How does that measure up to the accords being built with other faiths?"

I left the real question unsaid for now, no point in being too eager.

"The work of the order and the Holy Inquisition isn't as public as it once was. The battle against heresy concerns more about dangers of the faith from within the faithful, rather than direct competition with other religions. Although now hidden away from the public eye, the service we perform is still of vital importance."

I interrupted him again. "The Holy Inquisition?"

He paused for a minute before answering. "The Holy Inquisition is the more public face. They deal with the mundane heresies, such as books claiming that Jesus never died upon the cross and had a family of his own. They also keep an eye on the priesthood, to make sure that sermons are preaching the right message."

"And your order?"

"The Dominican order's battle against heresy is of a more secret nature. We contrast with the Jesuits who tend to deal with the more supernatural manifestations of evil." Wearing that weird smile he asked. "I'm sure you've seen The Exorcist?"

I nodded. Who hasn't?

"Well, that is their fight. They battle the Devil and his minions directly. The Dominicans deal with more human threats."

I'm not sure what I expected, but a history lesson of the Catholic Church hadn't been high on the list.

Friar Francis continued. "Combating heresy isn't just about preventing the corruption of the word of God. It's also about defending the faith from threats. Some of these threats are not just a problem for the church itself, but for mankind in general."

Now we were getting to it.

"Throughout history there have been individuals who possess abilities beyond what the secular authorities are equipped to handle. The church has spent the past two thousand years dealing with these dangers. In older times we could work openly with the authorities, but in this more secular age, discretion is required.

"Over the past few hundred years, secret accords have been established between the Vatican and many governments around the world. These arrangements allow the secular governments to pass along individuals that form a special type of threat."

"So I am one of these special threats?"

Again he unsettled me with the peculiar smile of his. "You are, but that isn't something we are going to discuss today. For now you just need to understand that the church has measures in place for dealing with people who have unique abilities. Abilities that make a regular prison a plaything for them. "

Again he flashed that odd little smile.

I felt thirsty again so I requested a drink of water, which Hammond provided. I drank the cupful in a single swallow and then asked, "So what happens now?"

"For now you are in our custody. There is no right of appeal and as we have demonstrated there is no way to use your powers to escape this prison. We have suitable people in place should you try a more mundane escape attempt." At this he pointed at Hammond looming behind me.

"There is, however, a way out for you. We won't speak of it yet. For now you will be taken back to your cell, allowed to sleep for the night and in the morning we will discuss things further."

Hammond brought some more water and the Friar placed two tablets in my hand. "Take these. They will help you sleep." I looked at them with suspicion, but what could I do? I could refuse, but I'm sure they would have just forced me to take them. This was not the time for confrontation, so I swallowed them.

Hammond returned me to my cell. "You would do well to listen to the Friar."

Thankfully my cell had been cleaned while in conversation with the Friar, so it no longer smelt like a pub toilet. The soundproofing here must be pretty good as I hadn't heard any cleaning, but it smelt and looked clean and that was good enough for now.

Against the far wall a cot had been placed with a thin mattress and some blankets. There was even a pillow. In the far corner a potty with a handle had also been provided.

Before closing the door the Friar said one last thing to me.

"What would you do for a chance at redemption?"

After he left, I slipped under the blankets, enjoying the feel and the warmth of them. For a while I pondered his question. Redemption, I know what the word meant, but it had no worth for me. As I fell into the haze of sleep I felt myself smiling.

Redemption? They were going to have to do better than that.

Chapter 23
We are the champions

I awoke feeling refreshed and ready for the day. That in itself made for a nice change. I still felt hungry, the bowl of soup the night before only allaying the intense hunger for awhile. I relieved myself into the plastic pot. I didn't like having to hold something you have to piss into, but what can you do? The splash back onto my hand that held the pot and the smell right under your nose was not the most pleasant thing to have first thing in the morning.

Still, the feeling of relief once my bladder drained more than made up for it and at least I no longer had to sleep in it. After replacing the lid I lay back on the bed and pondered what little information the Friar had provided the day before.

Obviously he wanted me to do something. The mention of redemption hinted that there was an action I could perform to earn their forgiveness. I thought the Friar would have been smarter than that, but I guess faith really can be blinding. Forgiveness as a concept that possessed no real meaning for me. To want forgiveness, I would assume that one would require guilt first. I hadn't experienced guilt for many years and regrets were most definitely not something I burdened myself with.

The only other thing I inferred was that if they needed me to do something, then that meant it required my specialist talents. Maybe they wanted me to deal with someone with abilities like mine. Fuck forgiveness, but a challenge, now that could be interesting.

An hour meandered by before the door opened and Hammond motioned for me to empty the piss-pot. After I emptied it, I washed my hands and face and then followed him into the other room. The Friar sat waiting for me with a cooked breakfast set out on the table. He invited me to eat. I happily obliged and tucked into this fine breakfast.

Sausage, bacon, a couple of fried eggs and some baked beans were artfully arranged on the white plate. All washed down with a mug of sweet tea. The menu might have been the same, but the quality far exceeded the last prison I had eaten in. When I finished, I leant back in the chair, satisfied. My hunger finally sated, for a while at least.

Friar Francis didn't speak a word while I ate, just sat there and watched. A little strange, but I don't like to talk and eat so he was welcome to stare at me if that amused him. When I finished he produced a packet of cigarettes from his robes. He lit one and then offered me the packet. I didn't normally smoke, not tobacco at any rate, but that day I felt indulgent. The smoke tasted harsh at first when I inhaled. I almost choked, but I managed to suppress the cough and then just enjoyed the acrid taste.

Sometimes the simplest pleasures are the best.

"You remember yesterday I spoke of the mission of my order? Our duty is to protect the church and its flock from people with unusual talents."

I nodded. "People like me."

There it was again, that little smile.

"No, not quite like you. There are two kinds of people with power: those who are born with it and those who develop it. Anybody who takes the time and has the discipline can develop abilities. It's not easy and often takes years of devotion, but it can be learned."

I assumed I fell into the born with it camp — after all, my mother never taught me anything about it. I paused for a moment. I hadn't thought of my mother for a very long time.

I know from the look of sympathy that he glimpsed my thoughts.

"There are those that are born with the gift. Such people are rare and they have the natural ability to apply their mind to affect the world around them. Even though they are born with this natural gift, it still takes training and effort to develop those powers."

"Rarer still are those we call Champions. Only a few are born in each generation. Their power is immense. Even without training they can bend those around them to their will. They are capable of feats unmatched by those with years of devoted training."

This time he nodded in confirmation.

"The Champions have existed as long as the church has existed, probably even longer. They each have a purpose, a destiny beyond that of a normal man. They exist for one purpose: the Celestial Conflict.

"For many years, both the church and the opposition have searched out these Champions to recruit them to their respective cause. Even without training they are capable of great deeds.

"In recent years, with the smaller numbers of the faithful some Champions have gone unfound by either side and grow to develop their talents without guidance. Individuals like you."

Hold on a minute, I thought, let's back-up a bit. "The Celestial Conflict?"

"Everyone knows the tale of the Eternal War," he answered. "The war that was started by Lucifer's sin of pride and defiance of God. The war that began long before mankind even existed. The war that tore the Heavenly Host in two and saw Heaven transformed into a battlefield until the Archangel Michael, as commander of God's armies cast Lucifer and his legions into Hell."

I couldn't help but smile at this, but the Friar ignored my silent mockery. "The war spread to the Earth after its creation, when Eve succumbed to temptation by Lucifer in the guise of a serpent. When she and her husband Adam gave in to that temptation, they caused the fall of man. Here on Earth the war has continued throughout history and will continue to do so until the End of Days. The Apocalypse."

Well I'd always known that people believed this stuff, but I had never met anyone who *really* believed it. I couldn't see into his mind, but by his very bearing I knew that he accepted what he told me as fact. I didn't really know what to say. This was beyond anything I had ever experienced. Even back then I had seen many things, some of them strange. But nothing I'd seen ever indicated this eternal struggle taking place in our world. My natural inclination was to mock him, to challenge those ridiculous beliefs. Instead I just asked, "What has this to do with me?"

He took his time in responding. "That's a fair question. Throughout history the Champions are raised by one side or the other, battling good or evil to help bring the end times and the final battle. As a Champion you must choose a side."

I actually laughed a little. "What choice?" I asked him. "I'm imprisoned here, at your command. What choice do I really have?"

I'm favoured with that strange smile again. "There is always a choice. You can choose to fight beside us. You can choose to return to your cell."

"As I say, that's not really a choice at all." Maybe there was a choice within a choice. "What is it you want me to do? To battle the Devil and all his minions?" I couldn't help it, I smiled again as I asked the question. It all sounded too fanciful.

"No, not Satan, or even his minions. Not yet. The church has a more immediate foe that needs to be dealt with."

That confused me. "That doesn't make any sense. You've just told me about this great war — a war that's lasted longer than history. The war that Champions are born to fight. What foe can be greater than that?"

When he lit another cigarette, I joined him. He asked me if I remembered the cold war. I did remember it. The threat of nuclear war was an ever present fear in my childhood. "Here were two great superpowers, each with enough firepower to annihilate all of mankind if they ever went to war. Heaven and Hell are in a similar predicament. Since the first battle they've skirmished for longer than the universe has existed. When the final battle comes, it will be one of annihilation. One side will win. The other will be completely destroyed. Neither side is in a hurry to see that happen, so the war continues, but each side is careful not to push too far, so they don't trigger the Apocalypse.

"As with the Cold War it wasn't Russia that was America's most dangerous foe. It was the believers; the fanatics that just wanted to see the other side destroyed and didn't care if they died with them."

"Like terrorists?" I asked.

"Exactly. We've faced a terrorist of our own for nearly two thousand years. A fanatic who will stop at nothing to destroy the church and all it represents. It's not the Devil we need you to fight. We need you to kill one of Jesus' first disciples, the very man he himself raised from the dead.

"We need you to kill Lazarus of Bethany."

Chapter 24
A man reborn

"Lazarus. You mean guy from the bible? The man Jesus resurrected from the dead? He's still alive and you want me to kill him?" I found it difficult to accept that I even had to ask these questions. Returning to my cell to escape this lunacy suddenly seemed like the sensible option.

Friar Francis didn't smile this time. His face wore a frown as he fiddled with the wooden cross that hung from his neck. He nodded in mute response to my questions. I was far from satisfied with this taciturn response.

"How can he still be alive? How is that possible? That would make him over two thousand years old!" A thought occurred to me, now there was a real power.

Again the Friar nodded.

This man infuriated me! "And you're trying to tell me that this person, raised from the dead by Jesus himself is a threat to the church?" Again I chuckled. "That doesn't make any sense. The bible doesn't even hint that Lazarus was an enemy of Christ. Why would he raise him from the dead if that were the case?"

Friar Francis sighed. "Not all truths are revealed in the Bible. There are some truths that must remain secret, for the good of all."

"I see." I didn't. "What I don't understand is how this could have been kept secret for all this time."

"Revealing the truth wasn't in the church's interest, or in Lazarus'. His purpose wasn't — isn't — to seek fame, but the destruction of the church."

When he lit another cigarette, I did the same. My throat felt a little raw, but the cigarette seemed the only sensible thing in the room at that moment. Hammond appeared from nowhere and placed two cups of tea on the table before he faded into the background once again. He didn't wear the mantle of servant well, but he managed it with grace. And silence. The man moved like a cat, impressive considering his size.

"To understand I suppose you should hear the story from the beginning."

I dragged on the cigarette and leant back, inviting the Friar to continue.

"Lazarus was a close friend of Jesus who lived in Bethany, a small town near Jerusalem. He became an active follower and one of the earliest disciples when Jesus first began his ministry. He usually travelled with Jesus. One day he had been called home for an emergency. It isn't clear what happened — some stories say that Lazarus was taken ill with a fever, others that he was involved in some altercation in which he had been gravely wounded."

"Altercation? Why would a disciple of Jesus involve himself in an altercation? Weren't they all about peace and love and turning the other cheek?"

"The original Christian movement was a little more militant than commonly believed. Anyway, it doesn't really matter. The point is that he was dying and his sisters Mary and Martha feared that he wouldn't survive the night. They called for Jesus to come as quickly as he could. Despite their urgent messages, two days passed before he started his journey to Bethany.

"When he finally arrived, Lazarus had already been dead for four days. The Gospel of John tells us that Jesus encountered Martha as he arrived in the town. She lamented with him, saying that he arrived too late and told him that his close friend was dead. Arriving at the home of Lazarus, they met Mary who was beside herself with grief. Beset with sorrow himself, he wept with the two sisters.

"They took him to the tomb where Lazarus had been laid to rest. At the tomb they encountered a large crowd, also mourning his death. There was much agitation from the crowd and the sisters protested as Jesus rolled the great stone away from the tomb. He raised his arms to Heaven and with tears still in his eyes prayed to God Almighty. He looked into the gloom of the tomb and in a loud, firm voice called for Lazarus to come forth.

"A moment passed and to the amazement of the gathered mourners they saw movement inside the tomb. They also heard an echoing moan that some said sounded leaden with despair. When Lazarus stumbled into view the crowd rejoiced and some fell to their knees, praising God and Jesus as his messenger. Jesus instructed the sisters to remove the grave linens and to let him be clothed as a living man, not as one of the dead."

"Way to go Jesus!" I interrupted. "That's very impressive. He sure knew how to work a crowd."

This time it was my smile that annoyed him: a petty victory, but a victory nonetheless.

"After this Lazarus resumed his travels with Jesus, working with him to preach the Gospel wherever they went. Unknown to Jesus, Lazarus carried a terrible desire in his heart. He had witnessed the glory of Heaven. More than that, he had dwelt there. In the four days that passed for his grief stricken friends and family, he had been taken into the bosom of God.

"Surrounded by a splendour only imagined of here on Earth, he lived amongst the saints and the angels. He conversed with the prophets of his people, heard their wisdom with his own ears. He sang with the choirs, praising the most holy. His voice joined in harmony with the blessed throng. Those four days were an eternity in paradise.

"And he was torn from this joy. Like a baby expelled from the womb he screamed his rage at the world he was dragged back into.

"Lazarus realised that his yearnings were wrong and he felt shame for this desire within him. Jesus had performed a miracle and this miracle brought believers to his Messiah's cause. In this he felt some satisfaction; after all, he had devoted his life to Jesus and his teachings."

The Friar paused, crushed out the remnants of his cigarette.

"He travelled with Jesus for months before they next returned to Bethany and his family. Together they celebrated with a meal, six days before Passover. After the meal he sat alone with Jesus and finally confessed the feeling of despair he suffered every day since his resurrection. Jesus took his hand and tried to comfort him by saying that God had a plan for everyone — that God's love knew no limit, no boundary. Even on earth it was still there if he would just accept it. In time Lazarus would return to Heaven and they would all be there together. He just had to follow the word."

"I can see that would annoy poor old Lazarus. It would annoy the piss out of me."

The Friar didn't rise to the bait this time.

"Lazarus tried to take comfort from those words, knowing that he was part of God's plan. But the words were hollow, just like the emptiness he experienced since his return.

"The Last Supper took place soon after. This meal was the last time before the crucifixion that Jesus and his disciples congregated. Lazarus sat beside Jesus, in the place of honour. But he could not engage with his closest of friends. He felt apart from them. He watched as Judas slipped out to earn his silver. He heard, but did not listen as Jesus bade them all farewell and predicted the denial of Peter. Like Judas he slipped away before the meal concluded.

"On the day of the crucifixion he followed the procession. He watched as the crowd, encouraged by the Roman guards, heckled and abused his Messiah. Unfortunately it was only his own loss that weighed in his heart. Halfway to the hill, the place of his execution, Jesus stopped by a shoe-makers shop. The cross was heavy. A burden almost too heavy for him to bear. He knew that soon he would die. In this moment of human weakness he turned to his friend looking for solace.

"Lazarus begged Jesus to allow him to ascend to Heaven together. Jesus, showing a rare moment of anger responded to Lazarus' presumption and cursed him: "As I witnessed your resurrection, so you must witness mine. Only then can we be joined in Heaven together." With those words, he shouldered the cross, the cross that was weighed not only with his impending doom, but with the sins of the world. And he climbed the hill."

I actually resisted the temptation to scoff.

"Feeling only despair and abandoning the shreds of faith that remained within him, he turned away from

Jesus, refusing to witness the death that would bring salvation to all. As many men do in their times of weakness he turned to wine to ease his torment. He spent many days in a stupor, complaining bitterly to those that would listen of his woes.

"He finally sought out the other disciples and to his shock saw that Jesus was alive, that he too had been resurrected. The crowd of apostles parted as he staggered towards Jesus, stinking of wine and shame. Jesus looked at him sternly. "I required one thing from you. I commanded you to witness my resurrection as I witnessed yours and together we would open the gates of Heaven. You denied me, ignored me and now you are condemned to walk the Earth until I return for the second time for the final judgement.

"Lazarus fell on to his knees before Jesus and wept."

Chapter 25
Scourge of the church

Friar Francis paused and lit another cigarette. It's impolite to make a man smoke alone, and so I lit one too. I'd only drunk half of my cup of tea, the rest now sat cold. At an unspoken command from the Friar, Hammond served us both fresh cups. A mess of congealed egg and cigarette ash covered my breakfast plate. I didn't say a word. We enjoyed a brief smoke in silence before he continued the story.

"In the time until Jesus ascended into Heaven Lazarus begged him for forgiveness. He pleaded with Jesus to take him too. His pleas were to no avail. He would have to suffer his punishment and await Jesus' return for the final judgement."

"So much for forgiveness, eh Friar?"

"Forgiveness has to be earned. After the ascension, Lazarus tried to resume his work with the other disciples spreading the gospel. They refused to work alongside him knowing that he had been condemned by their Messiah.

"Ostracized, Lazarus faded into the background and spent more time at home, hiding himself away with his sisters and their families. The years passed by and they too aged. Not knowing of Jesus' judgement, everyone remarked at how blessed Lazarus was to retain his youth. To him it sounded a bitter compliment."

"He should have moved," I interrupted the Friar again. "Moved to somewhere new, where he wasn't known."

The Friar nodded. "From your perspective I can see how that would have been the sensible course of action. For Lazarus, though, his sisters were all that remained of his former life. He felt abandoned and alone. Eventually though, his sisters died, and he still had not aged a day. Before his eyes they both withered away, became wrinkled and feeble. Over the years the congratulations of his blessings twisted as his circle of friends and family dwindled. Now he only heard mutterings of fear. The locals now considered him a fair faced monster. He was deemed unnatural and unwelcome.

"The whispers finally drove him from his home, now an empty sad place. For three hundred years no-one really knows where he went, or how he spent his time. There were rumours that he visited with mystics in the East. At first he hunted for a way to end his suffering. Later, when this quest failed, he sought to develop powers that eventually made him the threat we currently face."

To me that made Lazarus a fellow traveller, another being seeking escape from this rock. Interesting, but nothing more than that.

"This is what makes Lazarus so dangerous. As a mortal he was charismatic and full of vigour, but still just a mortal. There's only so much that can be learned in our short lives. In thirty lifetimes he has amassed a vast wealth of knowledge and developed his powers to a remarkable level, beyond that even of the Champions in some aspects."

That made him stronger than me. Until recently that would have shocked me, but after recent events I learned differently. Sometimes guile must be used rather than strength. I'm sure Lazarus understood the same thing, or he'd be all over the news.

"Lazarus didn't come back into the notice of the world for three hundred years. It was no coincidence that he made his appearance in the Middle East and Europe around the time the Catholic Church formed."

The Friar paused again, collected his thoughts. "Those long years desolated his soul. He discovered nothing that could destroy the miracle inside him. He saw the fledgling church and hated it. He hated what it represented — or perhaps more accurately, who it represented. From that moment he dedicated his existence to the destruction of the church."

"That doesn't seem such a bad goal to me."

"Then you don't know your history very well. The church has provided a stabilising influence for centuries. We were a bastion of learning when none other existed in Europe. The world would be a much darker place than it already is without its constant vigilance."

I could tell I had struck a nerve. Sadly my comment was just a barb. I wasn't one for book learning, despite the fact that I enjoyed reading. Maybe I should have paid closer attention to those dull history lessons. I mentally shrugged, or maybe not.

"At first his attacks proved relatively minor. He stirred up the locals against the new church and its priests, but soon escalated his activities and took to murdering isolated members of the church. The more important his victims the better. His existence and actions presented an embarrassment for the early church. The legend of his resurrection was too well known an act to hide, so that was kept in the gospels, but they expunged all other mention of his work with Jesus.

"For a while Lazarus maintained his identity, but he soon realised this made him too obvious a target. Wherever he appeared the church reacted quickly. He found himself hunted. Church forces even managed to capture him on a few occasions. Of course he could not be killed, but on one occasion his captors bricked him into the walls of a church. After thirty years he finally escaped this prison when some of his allies located him. Thirty years bricked up in the darkness, every day the torment of hunger and thirst further fuelling his hatred."

"I can imagine. That would piss me off too."

"Indeed, those long years trapped in the wall, with just the muffled prayers and sounds of the despised mass for company provided him the time to think. He changed how he operated and began to work through others more. He also travelled more widely. Wherever the church's missionaries journeyed, he followed. He supported the established religions, helped them resist. He enjoyed some successes, but even with a growing network he couldn't stop the tide of Christianity pouring across Europe.

"His first major success came from the followers of another youthful religion. He joined forces with some of the more energetic followers of Islam, aiding them in their invasion of the Holy Land. In response the Vatican and the European kings embarked on the Crusades. This sparked a terrible war that lasted for three hundred years and saw the Christians driven from the Holy Land.

"This was a major defeat for the Vatican. Lazarus tried to capitalize on it by encouraging his allies to invade Europe. Unfortunately for him the leaders of the Muslim forces saw no advantage in this. They had defeated the crusading armies only after many battles and at great cost. To take the war to Europe, especially to strike at the heart of the church, would cost too much. They risked losing everything they had so recently won.

"Again Lazarus adapted and developed a new strategy. This time he created or supported schisms within the church. All over Europe he provided funds and aid for heresies, most of which were quickly crushed through brutal action from the church. Some survived, but none were strong enough to substantially damage the church.

"For centuries he continued this guerrilla campaign using any means to strike at the church. While he caused many casualties, he never managed to match the success of the crusades defeat. Lazarus continued to develop his abilities and to expand his international network. Occasionally the Inquisition or the order tracked him down, although they never managed to capture him again."

Such a shame.

"This lack of meaningful progress became a source of great frustration for Lazarus and in recent years his strategy has changed again. He decided to give up the hit and run attacks, except as a diversion for his main assault. Instead he now planned to strike directly at the heart of the church. He planned to detonate a nuclear device at the Vatican during the Easter service. This would destroy Vatican City and the spiritual heart of the church. It would also devastate most of Rome and would likely cause a new war in the Middle East."

I really can't help but admire the balls of the guy. He thinks big. I'll admit I did feel a little envious. Don't worry, it soon passed.

"With his own network and contacts in various terrorist groups he arranged to steal a nuclear warhead in Pakistan. The Syrian Defence Intelligence Agency caught wind of the plot through their own contacts in the terrorist groups that helped to transport and steal the weapon.

"While relations between Syria and the West and the Vatican in particular weren't exactly cordial, it wasn't in their interests to see a nuclear bomb detonated in the centre of Rome. They passed the information onto Mossad through intermediaries. Mossad and the order intercepted the weapon and in the process captured or killed a large number of Lazarus' network. Lazarus himself managed to escape the operation."

"So job done then? Lazarus made his end run and it failed."

"Not quite," The Friar replied. "We stopped this attack and seriously wounded his operations. Indeed, it was a major victory."

Another pause, you could sense the but approaching.

"But unfortunately Lazarus shifted his strategy in response. He knows that his curse will be lifted when Jesus returns to Earth for the final judgement. To make that happen, he needs to trigger the Apocalypse."

Chapter 26
Stopping Armageddon

On that happy note we stopped for lunch. Hammond played mother again and brought me a tray of sandwiches, biscuits and a bottle of fruit juice. He and Friar Francis then left me alone with my thoughts while I ate. I heard the door lock after it closed.

I chewed through the meal slowly, savouring the taste as I thought about what the Friar had told me. He'd told the story well and I'd found myself caught up with it. Now I had time to think, I wasn't sure I believed what I'd heard. I thought it more likely that Lazarus was a title that passed down through the ages. I imagined the history of the early church was fraught with rivalries. Perhaps Lazarus was the leader, or the inspiration for one of those early sects. They had been one of the many losers and sustained a grudge that lasted throughout the centuries.

I thought that scenario more logical, more acceptable. However it didn't explain why they needed me to stop this person. Maybe this person was also a Champion? That helped balance it a little, but even so, they still wouldn't need me. I was still mortal and I assumed the other Champions were the same, so a bullet to the head would do the job just fine.

It was evident that this enemy represented a big deal to the Friar and the church. Big enough that they wanted me, a not-quite-convicted killer to do the job for them. With people like Hammond working for them, they didn't need me for the killing part. They required my specialist talents.

Satisfied with my conclusions, I washed the food down with the juice. They must have been watching me, as barely a minute later the door opened. The Friar entered, followed by Hammond who quickly cleared away the remnants of my lunch from the table. I tried to offer him a tip, but of course my pockets were empty. He scowled at my little joke.

The Friar sat down opposite me again, placed an ash tray on the table, lit a cigarette and offered the packet to me. This time I refused with a simple shake of the head. I know it was rude of me, but I've never been a big smoker. I began the conversation with a question.

"So how does Lazarus intend to kick start the Apocalypse?"

He smoked half of the cigarette before replying.

"For the Apocalypse to begin there are a number events that must take place. A sequence that signifies both sides are ready and willing to begin the final battle. There are various prophecies that provide a guide for each side for the events that they must complete."

He finished his cigarette and ground it out in the ash tray.

"It's an all or nothing play from Lazarus. If he pulls it off then it's the end of everything as we know it and he gets the confrontation with Jesus that he seeks."

This struck me as odd. "I'm seeing a flaw in his plan. His last confrontation with Jesus didn't end so well. Why would this time be any different for him?"

"He's taking advantage of what you would probably call a loophole. Each side's prophecies are meant to be completed by an individual representing them. Once the prophecies are complete the person who completed the event receives a specific power. If Lazarus completes all of the events himself he gains all of these powers. With these powers he may be a match for Jesus Christ himself."

Now that interested me. I wanted to know more. "How can that be so?"

He pondered for a moment. I couldn't see through the barrier around his mind, but I guessed what he was thinking. How much should he tell me?

"The pantheon of both sides has a hierarchy. At the top of the tree are the archangels, or arch-demons for the other side, but that's just semantics. Each archangel represents a different power, for example the Archangel Michael is God's Champion. He is the commander of Heaven's armies. By completing his set of prophecies Lazarus would gain the same power as the archangel Michael. By completing all of the prophecies he gains the power of all of the archangels. And those of the arch-demons as well."

"And that would make him stronger than the Son of God?"

"It would. The totality of his power would be beyond that of any single being."

"So why doesn't God stop him?"

Again he paused. "That's a good question, but you might as well ask why God allows anything? God created the universe to his own design, for a purpose not yet known to us. What we do know is that we have to follow his plan to the best of our abilities."

An unsatisfactory answer. Maybe faith made it more palatable.

"It does however present us with an opportunity."

I leant forwards. "How so?"

"Some of these events have to occur in specific locations. And some of these locations are in remote areas that are easily monitored."

"I doubt that Lazarus would show up to one of these places in person," I interrupted him.

"A year ago that would be the case. Now with most of his network dead or secluded in secret prisons all over the Middle East he has few resources to call on. And some of these events require actions that couldn't be entrusted to strangers or mercenaries. Anyway, he needs to complete the events in person to gain the powers."

"I see the possibilities that presents."

I'd not seen that odd little smile of his for a while.

"Let me be clear — I am not going to give you details of how to start the Apocalypse or for you to have a chance to gain these powers. We want you to do a job for us. It is an important job, but some secrets will not be shared with you. We haven't forgotten who you are or what you have done. We will tell you what you need to know and we will be closely monitoring you every step of the way. Do you understand?"

I accepted the chastisement with good grace. "I understand, but this is a new world you've brought me into. I need to know what makes this guy tick if I'm to hunt him and kill him for you. I need to know how to find him."

"We don't need you to find him. As I said, there are places he or someone close to him will need to go. We have all of these locations under surveillance. We will track him from there. The problem we have is taking him down when we do locate him."

"Ok, so have you spotted him yet? Has there been any activity at any of these mysterious places?"

"Not yet," he replied.

"What about the other events that he needs to make happen? Do you know if he has achieved any of them yet?"

Again he paused. That answered the question for me.

"Never mind," I told him. "He obviously has. So, the real question now is how close he is to completing these events?"

Another little pause before he admitted, "We don't really know."

And then it struck me. "The other side … you don't know what they need to do?"

"Not everything. We do have some contact with them, for diplomatic purposes. The Vatican and the Order stores some of their prophecies in our libraries. They're not complete, so we don't have a full understanding of what events their side need to do. And even with the little contact we have, they're not telling us. I think they believe we might be behind Lazarus' move."

"Ok then, if we assume that he has completed most if not all of their prophecies, then how close is he? He'll leave the difficult ones for last, knowing that with fixed locations there'll be traps. He'll plan for that."

There's a look that flickered across his face. I sensed an impending confession. I savoured the moment of irony.

"He has already completed one of the tasks at one of these locations. He managed to kill the team we had watching the church in question. He completed the sacrifice he needed to make. If he has completed the prophecies of Lucifer then he has five events left to complete. We have teams at each location."

I didn't bother to hide the smirk. "Are these teams better than the one that got wiped out?"

"We've reinforced the teams, but none of our operatives are capable of taking Lazarus on their own. That's why we need you."

And so we got down to it.

Chapter 27
A choice to be made

This time I helped myself to a cigarette. After lighting it I inhaled deeply and held the smoke in my lungs, extending that moment by delving into myself. I used this trick to give myself some extra time to think. We had finally come to it. Should I jump on board the crazy express? Should I follow this monk down his rabbit hole and kill this immortal man who held a grudge against everyone and everything?

I didn't have a problem with murder — my list was already substantial. At the crux of the matter though, was the question of if I wanted to get involved. If I wanted to see the outside of this cell then I would have to play along. They would watch me closely of course, but in the outside world, opportunities would occur.

Easy agreement would make them suspicious. Besides, if they needed me so badly, I was sure they would sweeten the deal. I held the smoke in my lungs for so long I experienced a mild head rush when I finally breathed out.

"So you want me to kill this Lazarus for you."

He nodded, lit another cigarette for himself.

"A man your people have been hunting for two thousand years. You've told me that they managed to capture him once, but couldn't kill him. The best they could do was brick him in a wall and all that did was piss him off even more. So my question to you is how can I kill him? Can he even be harmed?"

I decided to start keeping count of those little smiles of his. I had to admit, they were more than a little creepy.

"Lazarus is immortal, or at least very long-lived, but he's not invulnerable. He can heal any damage he suffers remarkably quickly. Mundane weapons can hurt him, but not kill him."

"Would a nuke kill him?"

He wasn't expecting that. "Are you serious?"

"Of course I am. At Hiroshima and Nagasaki I read there were just shadows left of some of the victims. They were vaporised by the blast. I think it would be pretty difficult to heal from that."

That wiped that annoying smile from his face. Besides, to save the world what cost a few thousand lives?

"I have no idea whether it would work or not and it is not an option."

"Are you sure? You did say that some of these locations are remote. I'm sure a small nuke would do the job."

"It is not an option. It would attract too much attention and probably wouldn't work anyway." The reply was emphatic. "To kill him you need to make him mortal. To make him mortal you will need to find and destroy the miracle inside him."

I should have expected something like that — that's why they needed me. "How do I do that?"

"The miracle is part of him. You need to break into his mind and find the miracle and destroy it completely."

"Do you know this for sure? Or are you just guessing?"

"We are certain. We have dealt with similar cases in this way."

"So why haven't you done the same with Lazarus?"

"His mind is phenomenal. The power and complexity of it is beyond what even our best people have ever gone against. Over the years he's turned his mind into a fortress — he'd have to be dead for his defences to be weak enough for one of us to get in."

That gave me an idea, but I kept it to myself.

"There is another complication," he continued. "The miracle is a divine thing. It can only be destroyed by a hand that has known evil."

Two points in my favour, although I'd never really considered myself evil before.

"Ok, so you really need me to do this for you. And I'm willing to admit that it might be fun, but what do I get out of it?"

He'd been expecting this question.

"By helping us you'll get the chance to see the world outside of these walls again. You'll be supervised every step of the way of course — we're not stupid. And by helping us you're also helping your immortal soul."

I couldn't believe he actually tried that line with me. I shook my head in wonder at his optimism. "Friar, you are really going to have to do better than that. Seeing the outside world is a good start. But trying to feed me the forgiveness line just doesn't cut it. I don't believe in your God or his Heaven, so his forgiveness has no meaning for me. I'm not even sure I even believe what you want me to do for you."

There was that fucking smile again and then realisation hit me. It was a test. With that understanding I returned him a little smile. Well played, sir.

"Good. If you'd suddenly converted I would have been more than a little suspicious. One day I hope you'll see the light, but for now we have more important issues. You'll be doing a good thing. You'll be saving the world and thus saving yourself."

"Saving myself for what? To sit in this cell for the rest of my natural born? Do you know why I was in prison in the first place?"

"I do. You hurt a lot of people."

"No, that's why others wanted me in prison. I went there to die."

If he smiled again I might have to cut his lips off.

"You didn't go there to die. You went there to make a statement. If you wanted to die you would have let the police shoot you at the scene. Bang, all over. You wanted people to know you, to fear you. You wanted recognition.

"I am not going to promise you things that I can't deliver to get you to do this for us. I also know that I can't appeal to your better nature — not that you don't have one, for there is one buried under all that bravado. You just don't realise it."

I said nothing, there seemed no point.

"What I can promise you is that you'll never get this opportunity again. Whether you like it or not you are here to stay. You have a chance here to spend a little time in the outside world again. You can also do something no-one else in the world can do. It's true that the world won't know what you did. But you will know, I will know, we will know. You'll become part of the secret history of the world."

A little flattery goes a long way, but this wasn't enough. I would happily kill this Lazarus, but I didn't care if he lived either. The only power I had was this choice and I knew the Friar worried that I would refuse. I didn't need to read minds to know that. He worried that I didn't care enough about anything to do this and I liked that feeling.

"I'll think about it," I told him.

He stood up. "You have tonight to think it over. In the morning you have to make your decision." Hammond appeared beside me and guided me back to my cell. As I left I turned to the Friar.

"Hey, if I say no, you can always try nuking him."

I slept well that night.

Chapter 28
Refusal often offends

The following morning I made my decision. I waited until finishing breakfast before telling them. As usual the Friar sat opposite me, but his weird smile soon turned upside down when I looked him in the eye and told him. "Friar, I've thought your offer over long and hard. In fact I hardly slept at all last night, but I'm afraid I can't kill this man for you. It just isn't worth the effort."

The Friar looked at me. "I suppose this is where I make you a better offer?"

"It can't hurt." I smiled.

"So are you saying that you are willing to do this, we just need to agree a price?"

"Make me an offer and we'll see."

He leaned back in his chair. "Let me see, what would interest you. Money?" He shook his head. "No, money is no good if you can't spend it. Instead of playing this game, why don't you tell me what you want?"

"But Friar, the game is the fun bit. All right." I held up a placating hand. "My price is simple. I kill this Lazarus for you and in return you set me free."

"That can't happen I'm afraid. You are too dangerous to be let loose in the world."

"More dangerous than letting Lazarus kick-start the Apocalypse?"

"A fair point, but unfortunately we've already agreed with the British government to keep you locked away and safe."

"That's a shame. They wouldn't have to know. And doesn't saving the world count for more than a little legality?"

"It's not that simple I'm afraid."

"How complicated can it be? Six billion lives in exchange for my freedom."

"Our word is our bond. We cannot break that agreement."

"Sure you can. It's easy. Just open the door."

"You don't understand. We cannot break our oath. To do so would diminish us, and we need our strength. We cannot afford to lose any of it by releasing you."

I really didn't understand what he meant, and I couldn't have cared less either. As far as I was concerned this was some trick. A way for him to weasel out of giving me a better deal.

"However, there are prisons and there are prisons. Instead of a plain cell with no view of the outside world we could organise something more comfortable."

"Such as?"

"A secluded island in the Mediterranean. There's wonderful weather with a small villa and discreet guards. Enough diversions to keep you occupied for your stay there. There's also the opportunity for further work. Work that would get you into the outside world, if only for a short time."

I took my time finishing the sweet tea that accompanied breakfast while I thought about that offer.

"I'm afraid that isn't enough, Friar. I want proper freedom. Nothing less."

"We won't make this offer again. Are you sure this is your final decision?"

I smiled. If they really needed me to do this job then this was just a bluff. "I'm sure. I suppose this means I will be taken back to my cell?"

The Friar didn't say anything. Hammond stepped forward, ready in case I resisted. I allowed him to lead me back to the cell. And so began a new, if familiar routine.

I didn't see the Friar or Hammond again for several weeks. They moved me to a different cell. At least this one had some furniture: a metal framed bed, bolted to the floor and a chair also secured to the ground. This cell even had a toilet and a small sink. Meals were passed in by different guards through the slot in the door three times a day.

Every few days a quartet of guards, each armed with tazers escorted me to the shower room. In that time I never saw, or heard any other prisoners. I had the sense there were others, but no evidence.

I spent my time probing at the walls, always searching for a weakness I could exploit. I assumed they monitored my activities, for if I discovered a weakness it soon disappeared. I repeatedly asked for books, anything — even the Bible again. It wasn't a bad time, but I soon became bored. The guards never spoke to me, they simply ignored my requests.

As well as the walls I probed the guards. None had the ability to block me as the Friar could. As with Hammond they wouldn't try to resist, their minds an open book. At the centre of these minds I'd always find the rock. The rocks differed between each guard. Some large, some small. Different textures, different colours, always in the same place.

Only if I tried any action against the rocks would the guards react. That reaction usually meant a jab with their tazers. I quickly decided it wasn't worth the extra pain.

Thinking of the Friar made me wistful. To my surprise I actually missed the conversations. After several weeks it became clear I had miscalculated. Friar Francis didn't return with a better offer.

Chapter 29
Things that go bump in the night

The days blended into each other. I guess it must have been at least two months since being left in isolation when one night something disturbed me from my sleep. I didn't know what it was. One moment I slept, the next I awoke. Some sense alerted me to impending danger. Quietly I slipped out of bed and dressed in the loose trousers and jumper.

I suppressed the sudden flashback to the night of my first kill.

Straining my senses I searched for the source of the disturbance. I heard nothing. Already knowing it was a futile effort, I scanned the gloom of the cell anyway. Hunting for anything I could wield as a weapon. Experimentally I pulled at the chair, but its bolts held it secure to the floor. I cut my finger trying to turn the bolt. I tried the others hoping one would be loose.

A dull thud rocked the building. I gave up on the bolts and crouched by the door. The silence was ruptured by another explosion. This one sounded nearer. Powerless, I waited through the quiet that followed. Another minute passed before another explosion, this one even closer than the last. The floor shook slightly beneath my feet. Now I heard new sounds: what sounded like the crackle of gunfire, each shot creeping closer.

What the hell was going on?

The gun battle started as a few isolated shots quickly rose to a crescendo, then died away. I remained listening by the door. Eventually I heard quiet scuffs — men in boots sneaking? I didn't like the feel of this one bit. I gathered my will, prepared myself in case the door opened.

The footsteps stopped by my door. Again I looked around the shadows of the cell. No escape there. I had nowhere to hide and nowhere to run. Without flight, fight became my only option. A soft thud against the door. I stepped back. I heard a whispered voice. I stepped back again.

Suddenly I lay on the floor, and the door now flat on top of me. My ears rang from the blast, my head dazed. The smell of acrid smoke filled the cell. I tried to focus my eyes, but saw only a blurred vision of bright light in the doorway. Silhouettes of two men passed through the bright portal and strode beside me.

They pulled the weight of the door from me. The lifted weight revealed new pains. Even stunned I fought. I surged my will into the nearest man's skull. Shocked, I found that his mind had no substance — a murky swamp of poorly hidden secrets and desires. It reminded me of the minds of some of the younger prisoners. A montage of deceit and delusion, tinged red with cheap violence.

He possessed no defences and I tore through it with ease, wisps of his essence swirling around my being like mist. Then I understood that I couldn't grasp his thoughts. I flailed around, grasping, the smoke of his personality slipped through my will.

Never had I experienced anything like this, although before meeting the Friar I had never encountered anyone capable of blocking my will either. This was different, as if this man's mind had no substance. Another oddity occurred to me: this guy didn't seem to know that I had delved into his brain.

My eyes adjusted to the light from the doorway. Other figures waited impatiently by the door. Now I saw they were all uniformed in black, their forms bulked out by body armour and weapons. The two stood beside me dragged me to my feet. I stumbled, still dazed from the explosion. My ears still rang with a high pitched whine.

I assaulted the other man's mind. I found another world of smoke. An unexpected flash of memory from my life on the streets, crack head minds were like this. The chemicals shredded their thoughts, put them beyond any rationality.

Half carried, half dragged they removed me from the cell. In the corridor another six black-clad commandos waited, their weapons held ready. Four broke off and led the team to the gaping hole that was once a door.

Although I slowly regained my sensibilities, I kept myself slumped, making my new guards work at extracting me from this secret prison. Beyond the destroyed door I was pulled through what looked like a waiting room, with some comfortable chairs arranged around a low table. Along one wall stood a small kitchen area and a flat screen TV placed upon the neighbouring wall.

This must be where the guards spent their time. It looked almost as sad and lonely as my cell, although frankly I would have welcomed a TV. From this area we encountered a stairway. I was surprised when they started dragging me up the stairs. I had been kept underground all this time!

Through a trail of devastation they led me out to the open air. Despite the situation it felt good. The night breeze felt cool against my face. I snatched a quick glance at the sky above. Even in this desperate situation I marvelled at it. No light pollution marred the blackness. I saw no moon, only the jewels of stars above.

With my head now cleared I seized my chance. I elbowed the guard to my right. His body armour absorbed most of the blow, although the force still knocked him aside. I turned and struck the other guard in the face. He grunted in pain, but came straight back at me. He swung his rifle, I ducked just in time.

Expanding my awareness I spotted another guard as he charged me from behind. I twisted out of his reach only for the other guard's rifle to strike me in the back of the head. Bright light burst behind my eyes and I fell to my knees, immediately struggling to stand. Another blow landed and all turned to darkness.

Chapter 30
Not so pleased to meet you

Waking up after a beating seemed to be becoming a habit for me. As habits go, I'd enjoyed better. I moved my arms, and found them constrained by chains, indicated by the rattle of metal. More than that, the chains held me tight against a pole, in the middle of a large musty room.

I looked around, my head still sore and a little unbalanced. I saw nobody else. The room radiated a medieval vibe with its old worn stonework. Dust formed patterns on the floor, no furniture brightened the view. I couldn't see the door but I was willing to bet it was an iron-bound wooden one. The room smelled of dry decay as if an age had passed since it last held guests.

Unfortunately I didn't remain alone for long. The creak of ancient hinges heralded the arrival of someone. The door closed as noisily as it had opened. Absolute silence reigned for too long. I almost felt relief when I heard movement behind me.

Soft footsteps paced back and forth, never quite entering my limited sight. I struggled to turn and face whoever it was. I wanted to identify them, to know my captor. The chains locked me in place.

Unable to see the unknown person behind me I expanded my awareness to see with other eyes. These walls were infused with some power, similar to that which guarded the prison, forming a barrier I could not penetrate. Other than that I detected nothing, could see or feel no presence. Yet I clearly heard the footsteps behind me.

Breath touched my neck.

In that moment I remembered what fear tasted like. A long time had passed since I last experienced such a thing. I clearly recalled that lump in my chest the night I waited for my mother and then heard that knock at the door. The fear that gulped from my stomach, forced its way through my chest and into my throat.

Then I could do nothing. This time I was no young boy. I surged, slammed my will throughout the room and against the stone walls. It struck nothing, a wave crashing unimpeded against the sea wall. Like that dread moment, when as a boy I could do nothing.

"So this is the champion?"

A sibilant voice that crept along the edge of my hearing. It caressed my thoughts. Did I hear the voice? Or only imagine it? A cruel laugh again — sensed more than heard — and I guessed the identity of my tormentor.

"Lazarus I presume?"

"So you know me."

"I read about you in a book once."

"Funny, but you seem to have me at a disadvantage. You know me, but I don't know you?"

When you have nothing else, make sure to maintain appearances. Whatever happened I would not let this man witness my fear.

"You've gone to a lot of trouble to see somebody you don't know."

"When somebody is asked to kill me, I like to meet them. And it just so happens I have need of a champion."

"Are you going to offer me a job?"

"I'm afraid not. It's your blood I need. The rest of you is disposable."

"I see."

"I don't think you do, but no matter. I need your blood for a certain ritual. When I heard that the order had finally found a champion I couldn't believe my good fortune."

"I'm happy to oblige."

"And now I find you to be just a fledgling without a clue as to who you are or what you can do. Well. You can't imagine how happy that makes me."

I could imagine all too easily. He still paced behind me — I heard his movement. Again I focused. Still I saw nothing, detected nothing. Show yourself. And he did. Lazarus stepped into view.

At first glance he didn't appear out of the ordinary. He stood as tall as me, slightly heavier build maybe. His dark skinned face lined with age. He only looked like a modest age of forty or so, not the two thousand years the Friar claimed. A full beard and trimmed hair framed his face.

His suit appeared well cut and expensive, not that I'm any real judge of fashion. His eyes, though — they looked wrong. Dark and expressionless, they lacked shine. Those eyes offered an invitation, one that I readily and foolishly accepted. I gathered my will and dived straight in.

I encountered nothing. No mind at all, not even the barest of impulses. Nothing at all lay behind those eyes. And he smiled.

"You can't see me, can you?"

He chuckled again, a mockery that echoed through the chill room. "The Black Friars seek to stop me with an untalented boy like you." Another laugh. "They must be getting desperate."

"As it happens I refused the job."

"And I am supposed to be thankful for that? I think not."

I didn't understand how he could hide from me, not that it mattered. The fear that flared at his arrival was now a bitter thing. I couldn't allow myself to succumb to it. With an effort I swallowed it. I compressed that fear, let it fuel me. A false sneer edged my voice when I challenged him. "Brave words from a man who has me chained." Foolhardy to goad a man like this, but the tiniest of chances was surely better than none.

He smiled. I saw no warmth in that gloating grin.

"You are correct. This is most unseemly of me." With a curt gesture the chains fell in a pile at my feet. How did he do that? I started to wonder if maybe the Friar was right, but too late for that now.

Knowing that my ability wouldn't help me, I charged straight at him. No finesse, just a bull stampeding a rival. He caught me easily and threw me to the ground.

I sprang back to my feet as he closed and threw a hasty punch. He shifted his head enough to dodge the blow. His smile teased me, his movements smooth and unhurried. I threw another punch, this time he blocked it. The pattern repeated over and over. He casually blocked or evaded my blows. Eventually I realised that he could read my moves before I made them. His own thoughts remained hidden from me.

Dodging another punch he lunged forward and grabbed my throat. With a power that belied his stature he lifted me easily. It took all my strength just to breathe in his grip. "Don't worry, you won't suffer for long. I will perform the ritual tomorrow night. It will hurt and thanks to your innate ability you will get to enjoy every moment while I cut your beating heart from your chest. You'll die afterwards of course, but I'm sure you'll consider that a mercy."

"Fuck you."

Lazarus threw me against the wall, and then seized my face in his hands. His breath was warm, smelling innocuously of mints. An undercurrent subtly revolted me.

"Let me show you what you could not see."

With that he opened his mind. It exploded into being like a supernova in the night sky. What was once darkness now shone a light too bright for my comprehension. His mind slithered, a serpent of destruction that coiled around my own. I challenged my will against his. My anger and fear lent me strength. Not much, but enough to for me to hold out for a few more seconds.

The weight of his will was immense. Only now did I truly appreciate the truth of what the Friar said. The centuries added to his power, my own strength a mere candle to his. It gave me a moment of humility.

But only a moment.

I lashed back, driving into him with all my will, he swallowed me whole. All I heard was his laughter. The violence of it shredded my thoughts.

"Yes, you will make a fine sacrifice," were the last words I heard before returning to the darkness.

Chapter 31
A little show and tell

I was truly fucked. They left me in a heap on the cold stone floor, hardly the most dignified of wake ups. Lazarus obviously didn't consider me a threat, the locked door and ancient walls sufficient to contain me. With no windows I couldn't even guess at the time of day. I didn't know how long I had been knocked out. All I knew was that sometime soon I would be the sacrifice for some crazy ritual I didn't even believe in.

I didn't ache as much, but the stale taste of defeat soured my mouth. Throughout the discussions with the Friar, it never occurred to me that I couldn't do the job. The only question had been did I want to?

Well now I knew the answer to that question. I very much wanted to, but now doubted whether I could. That doubt hurt me more than any of the recent beatings. I gave myself a mental shake — no point dwelling on it. I needed to find a way out. If I could escape then maybe Lazarus had done me a favour after all.

I know, a pretty thin silver lining, but better than none at all.

It didn't take long to search the gloomy space. The door opened as I vainly pressed stones in the wall, my fantasy of finding a hidden door interrupted. Lazarus entered, flanked by two of those misty-minded guards.

Less forcefully than before I delved into Lazarus' mind. A barrier prevented entry, no great surprise there. It felt very different from the barrier that enclosed the room. That was solid and smooth. The one around his mind repulsed me. To the touch it coiled and squirmed, almost a living thing.

Lazarus wore that dead grin. Somehow it made me miss the Friar's smile. His eyes still looked lifeless. "Don't worry my boy. The time of your death is not quite upon us. For now I would like to ask you a few questions."

I noticed the guards each wielded a tazer, no doubt to subdue me with if I resisted. They would need them. "Why would I want to answer any questions?"

"Why, to save yourself unnecessary suffering of course." He seemed excited at the prospect. This is not right, I remember thinking. It is I who imposes suffering, not this myth made man stood before me.

The two guards secured an arm each. Lazarus stepped close, that minty breath violating my nostrils. Naturally I resisted, and predictably it proved futile. Lazarus clamped his hands against my face and in an almost gentle voice asked. "Let's start simple. Who was the Friar who recruited you?"

"I refused the job."

"You would have died either way. What was his name?"

"You know, I can't remember."

The pain came without warning. Fiery needles stabbed into my flesh all over my body. I used my will to prevent myself screaming. As suddenly as it started, it stopped.

"Let's try that again. What was the Friar's name?"

"You know, I don't think he told me."

Again the searing needles jabbed into my flesh. This time I was prepared and delved into myself, retreating from the wave of pain.

His voice echoed from a great distance. "There's no escape that way."

His hands reached into me, grasped for my fleeing essence. As those hands touched me I shuddered. His fingers sank into me like claws. Fresh agonies that I couldn't escape rippled through me.

"What was his name?"

"I can't remember."

Those words became my mantra. I focused on those three simple words. My world shrank to a single imperative. I would not answer that question. I didn't owe the Friar anything, but neither did I owe anything to Lazarus. And let's just say I don't react well to threats.

I don't know how long the torture lasted. It can't have been too long, maybe an hour. It's almost a cliché to say it felt like longer, but it was true nonetheless. The pain and the mantra required all my attention. I retreated further and further within myself. I'm certain I never uttered the Friar's name. I made sure not to even think it. At one point the pain became too much. The mantra of denial no longer provided enough of a diversion.

Instead I channelled that pain into anger. I would make this bastard pay. I didn't know how I would do it, but I would unleash my fury upon him. For a brief moment the pain stopped, and I opened my eyes in time to see the grimace flinch across his face. Somehow I had hurt him!

Only much later I worked out that Lazarus had sunk too deep inside me. By not considering me a threat, he left himself vulnerable. Inside my mind my will had teeth. My talent may have been woefully underdeveloped compared to his, but I had some natural strength. This time I smiled.

I caught the glance he aimed at one of the two guards, who rammed the tazer into my ribs. I collapsed convulsing to the floor. This new physical pain overwhelmed the memory of the previous psychic torture.

Lazarus loomed over me.

"Ok, let's do this the old fashioned way." He pulled a knife from a sheath concealed inside his jacket. The poor light reflected oddly from its curved blade. It looked as if the metal of the blade was corrupted with cruelty. With his other hand he grasped my throat, not enough to choke, just enough to hold me still. The guards pinned my arms to the ground.

With a delicate motion he sliced my cheek. The pain was nothing compared to the slowly fading echoes of the tazer shock. I bucked, heaving to shift his bulk off me. He sliced again, in exactly the same place, opening the cut further. The dampness of the blood felt warm on my check. It crept lower, snaking to my neck.

"I will strip the flesh from your bones. I only need you alive for the ritual, it doesn't stipulate in what condition you have to be in. Now what was the Friar's name?"

He punctuated each word of the question with another slice. Each cut a little deeper, the pain sharp as the blade that mutilated my face. From this physical pain I could have delved and found some escape, but then I would lose comprehension of what they were doing. I balled the pain inside me. It took a huge effort to hide it, but no way would I scream out for his pleasure. With a voice that wavered more than I would have liked, I denied the knowledge again.

A new slice, this time across the other cheek. Jesus would have been proud of me. My strength faltered. The next cut forced a cry from me. I snapped my mouth shut, stifled the scream, causing fresh pains to blossom.

More slices accompanied by the same question, over and over again. Blood poured down my cheeks. My struggles gradually weakened. Now with each cut I cried out. I no longer cared about revealing my weakness. I concentrated only on thoughts of revenge. I shouted the words of my imagined vengeance in defiance of each wave of pain.

All the while he smiled, enjoying my agonies. My screams were only a symphony for his delight. That smile shifted when the room trembled with a dull roar. His face blanked, concentration suddenly elsewhere. I seized the moment and resumed my struggle. Almost casually he punched me in the face, the blow tearing the cuts further. I howled, and the guards strained to hold me down.

Lazarus stood. My chest was happy to be relieved of his weight. "Watch him," he commanded and headed to the door. One of the guards jabbed the tazer into my side again, held it there for longer this time. My consciousness dimmed. The weight from my arms lifted allowing my convulsions to continue their dance unhampered.

Another explosion shook the room, dust drifted down from the ceiling. A feeling of déjà vu as I heard gunfire in the distance. The two guards looked worried as they realised that they were only armed with tazers.

I made my move as the door burst open. I crashed into the first guard. The other dropped from a controlled burst from a large black-clad figure framed by the doorway. Another burst shredded the face of the guard I wrestled with. I let his body drop to the floor.

Hammond pulled his face mask up, allowing me to recognise him. He scanned the room, satisfied it was clear then beckoned me to the door.

"It's a good job we implanted a tracker." A man of few words, but they were welcome words indeed. I followed him out to the corridor. We ran up some stone steps and entered an old chapel. Several dead guards littered the church floor. Other soldiers dressed like Hammond checked them for signs of life.

Friar Francis commanded the troops. He looked out of place in his black habit.

"Lazarus is not here. He must have escaped. Let's get out of here."

Hammond assisted to the waiting helicopter outside. I succumbed to the comforting darkness moments after it lifted off the ground.

Chapter 32
Learning to focus

The Friar allowed me to rest for several days after returning me to my old cell. They fed me well. They even let me have a book to read — the Bible again, although reading a book isn't as much fun when you already know how it ends. Hammond and the Friar took it in turns to debrief me. Amongst the questioning the Friar reassured me that they hadn't known that Lazarus needed a champion for a sacrifice. I didn't care; I only wanted revenge.

On the seventh morning we shared a breakfast and while eating the full English I pressed the Friar. "I'll do it. I will kill Lazarus for you. I want some revenge on that son of a bitch. When do we go?"

"Soon," He replied. "First we have to locate him and when we have Lazarus you can do your thing. In the meantime we have planning and you have much preparation to do."

I finished chewing the mouthful of egg and bacon, washing it down with a gulp of sweet tea. "True, I need some better tricks. I'll be ready for him next time."

Ah, that odd little smile again.

"You will be, but let's start simple. Before we get started I know what you are thinking."

That didn't surprise me.

"You are thinking that once you have the skills and inflicted your revenge you can then force your way out of our custody and break the deal."

I had indeed been thinking along those lines.

"You already know that we implanted a tracking device in your body, without which we couldn't have rescued you. The device is continuously monitored. No-one here knows where it has been placed. The people monitoring your location are at a different facility and we have no direct contact with them. Should they see you moving beyond the parameters that we allow then they will activate the device's secondary function.

"This time there will be no attempt to capture or restrain you. At the press of a button from half a world away the device will self-destruct, taking you with it."

I contemplated this for a minute and then nodded in understanding. There would be a workaround somewhere. I just had to find it.

The Friar read my mind again. "We know that you may be willing to take this chance, or even find a way to block the device. So from now on you will have to wear this."

Hammond placed a metal collar onto the table.

"Put it on."

"What is it?"

"A final piece of insurance. It's a shock collar. Act out of line and it'll put and electric shock through your neck. Not enough to kill you, but it will be enough to keep your mind busy for awhile."

I picked up the collar. It looked too thin to be a real threat, but I assumed that they wouldn't try to stop me with a placebo. Hammond, the ever present shadow, stood by my shoulder. I sensed his thoughts. As always he made no attempt to hide them. He almost wanted me to try something stupid.

"If you don't put it on then the deal is off."

The desire for revenge burned too brightly. I'd find a way round this new problem later, but for now I needed that training. I placed the collar around my neck. It snapped shut.

Another concern surfaced. The real danger would come when the job was finished. If they had no further need of me, then they would take me down immediately. Friar Francis wasn't stupid, so he would know that I suspected this. I think we both had interesting times ahead.

For now I complied with their terms. The Friar wasted no time and later that morning we began my training.

"To master the ability you have, you need to learn two things. The first is how to measure the power you project. You need to learn how to control it. The second is how you can use symbols to focus the ability.

"You're already on your way to mastering the first problem. In the time we've known you, the amount of force you put into your ability has changed. You've learned to probe, to tease before charging in with all your might. We'll help you develop that further. To do this we'll give you some items that you can practice with."

He placed a plain wooden box on the table in front of me. "Inside this box is an item. I want you to tell me what it is."

I looked at the box. The wood was polished to a rich dark sheen, but I couldn't see any ornamentation or markings of any kind on its surface. I reached forward to examine it and the Friar snapped a terse instruction. "Do not touch the box! Examine it only with your mind."

I leaned back and expanded my awareness, wrapped it around the box. I sensed the barrier that protected the box, fractionally larger than the box itself. I probed at the barrier, rippled my presence against it. It felt uniformly smooth on all sides. I pressed against it, probing for a weakness.

"I can see you have surrounded the box with your awareness. You can feel that it is a single shape. There are no gaps, or weaknesses. Try again to find a blemish."

With my focus acting like a finger I rubbed it along the barrier. Even along the edges it felt smooth.

For several minutes he watched me. "You're seeing things as you would with your eyes, they are big and clumsy. Focus only on feeling the barrier, but make the probe much smaller than your finger. Nothing is perfect — that is the nature of the universe — but it is the imperfection that you seek."

The probe from my mind shrank. I didn't look at the box. With my eyes closed I built a mental image of the box with only what sensed with the probe. It still felt as smooth as glass.

Again the Friar waited, allowing me to explore before offering guidance. "Focus smaller. Nothing is solid. There is a gap to be found in everything. The denser the shield, the smaller you need to become to find the gap. Once you have the gap you have found the weakness. Find the gap in the box."

I narrowed the probe further, making it even smaller. I reduced the focus so there wasn't a box, just an edge. I pushed in tight and there it was. A dimple, the tiniest fraction of the whole had a depression. I zoomed in tighter on this dip, a blemish smaller than the troughs on a CD. I found more dips, a vast array of them. The more I zoomed in, the more imperfections I discovered.

I picked at the tiny dips for some time, finally inspiration hit me. I created another probe alongside the original. I repeated the process until several probes were all touching the tiny faults. With the probes all in place I pushed. As I exerted, I focused the tips smaller while I poured more of myself into the prongs. I felt the skin of the barrier part. As it weakened I pressed in more probes. Then one of the probes pushed through. The physical box proved to be no impediment for my sight with the barrier gone. I was already smaller than the gaps between the box's atoms.

I poured my awareness into the box. It filled the volume within. Still I didn't look. I formed my awareness into a negative shape of the box's interior. I examined the shape of the impression.

"It is a cross, a silver cross with a roughly cast Christ hanging in his usual dreary torment."

He rewarded me with a smile. It almost looked genuine.

More time had passed than I realised, and we stopped for lunch. I had never focused my will in such a delicate fashion before. The strain caused a headache right between my eyes. In the afternoon the Friar set another exercise. He placed a new box, a fresh puzzle onto the table. This time I sensed a pattern in the barrier.

"This time you have to discern the pattern in the shield."

I followed what I learned that morning. I narrowed the probes and searched for the gaps. Finding the gaps proved easier this time, but I comprehended no pattern, only a chaotic mess. I pulled back, re-examined the problem. I assumed the pattern to be on the same level as the flaws in the shield. My assumption was flawed — that wouldn't make sense. The flaws were a natural thing, and the denser the barrier, the smaller the flaw. The pattern must be a deliberate thing. It wouldn't be at the same level.

I enfolded the whole box with my awareness. I subdivided the surface into probes, splitting them smaller and smaller. There were too many, I couldn't focus on each one. My thoughts became overwhelmed by the number of them. With a curse I lost my concentration.

"Don't try to control each probe, let it do its own job. Concentrate on the whole."

I tried again and pull backed, allowed the probes to keep dividing. I followed the advice from the Friar. When the probes found a gap they stopped dividing. Most were long and thin, and then I saw that some were shorter and wider. I withdrew the long probes, left only the shorter ones, and looked at the pattern.

"It's a fish. A fish symbol like you see on the back of God-botherers' cars."

I received another smile and another puzzle.

That evening I probed at the cell walls. I sensed multiple barriers, all meshed together. It would be difficult and time consuming to penetrate, but not impossible. I experienced less success on my hunt for the tracker implant. My head ached when I finally fell asleep.

Chapter 33
The power of symbols

I'd spent over a week working through those exercises. Friar Francis appeared to have an endless supply of puzzle boxes. Each presented a new aspect that I needed to discover. The puzzles grew ever more challenging, and that helped me develop new techniques for attacking each one.

In the evening when they left me to my own devices I continued to probe at the barriers that enclosed the cell. I think they monitored my progress. Every evening the structure of the entwined barriers changed. No doubt they considered it homework for my education. I continued this despite the pounding headache that developed by the end of each day. The daily changes made it a frustrating exercise, but at least it proved that the shield around the cell was vulnerable. Any weakness merited further investigation.

Finally Friar Francis introduced a new element in the training program. Before we started I asked him if there was any progress in locating Lazarus.

"Nothing concrete yet, but there has been some unusual activity near the site of an ancient temple on the island of Cyprus. There's been no direct sighting of Lazarus himself, but some strangers have been spotted in a nearby village. Luckily for us the area is remote, so anybody new stands out.

"If these are Lazarus' people we'll have to move out there soon, probably in the next few days. So we need to push things forward a bit faster than I'd like.

"Today we're going to shift focus. Before we started I said there were two things you needed to work on to become ready. You've been working pretty hard on the first issue and you've picked it up quickly, so I'm hoping you'll do the same with today's new subject — symbols."

I shouldn't have felt warmed by his praise, but I did.

"Symbols are a way of visualising the effect you are trying to achieve. For most people symbols provide the only mechanism for developing these abilities. Usually we start with learning how to leave your body, but I think we can skip that step with you."

I closed my eyes for a moment so I could avoid that smile. It was still there when I opened my eyes.

"Symbols provide a focus for what you think, or as a guide for what you want others to think. Let's start with a simple but very useful trick: how to make yourself invisible."

Cool.

"You're not actually invisible, of course. The affected people will just ignore you, so don't try using it against cameras."

Duly noted.

"Now expand your awareness and fill the room."

I did as he instructed.

"Now place the image of the room in your head. Don't worry too much about the little details, focus on the broad brush strokes — people will fill in the details for themselves. When you have the image fixed in your head, remove yourself from the picture."

I found this surprisingly difficult to do. Some part of me kept putting me back in sight. It was as if some secret part of me feared that removing myself from the picture would also remove me from reality.

Friar Francis understood my problem. "Instead of removing yourself from the picture, try painting yourself transparent. You're still there, you can just see through yourself."

That worked. I now had the room in my head, and I could see through myself.

"That's good. Now, expand your awareness again, this time carrying the picture with you. Let your picture of the room fill the room."

I repeated this several times until he was satisfied, then he instructed me to delve into Hammond's mind and look through his eyes. A moment later I looked through Hammond's eyes. It looked the same. I saw everything as it was.

The Friar chuckled. "You're too used to delving. Try looking through his eyes as filtered by his brain, not directly through the eyes." I did this and pulled back from Hammond's eyes and into his mind. I watched myself fade from view. Wow, cool trick.

"That's good. Now let's see you keep it up with more than one person." He walked to the door and after opening it he called down the hallway. For the remainder of the day different people, mostly guards, paraded through the room. As I delved into them I noticed that like Hammond they all had that monolith at the centre of their minds — the rock that anchored their thoughts. I suddenly realised that it represented their faith. Their faith centred them. That explained why each person's was different, a different look, a different size, but always in the same place.

Only people here seemed to have them. Although it would be fair to say I haven't mixed with many believers over the years.

On the few occasions the picture slipped, the Friar swiftly reprimanded me. I'd quickly recover and hold the image steady. With his guidance I learned that my mistake was trying to push the image into each person one by one. The trick was to hold the image clear in my mind and let it fill the room.

"You picked that up quickly. It can be very useful, but as I said it won't work against technology. Its other drawback is that it won't work with people who can shield their minds. Or rather it won't work if a person has their mind shielded."

All through the next day I continued to practice. A seemingly endless succession of people walked through my expanded awareness and they didn't see me. My head ached more than ever.

That evening, while we ate dinner, Friar Francis continued to lecture me about symbols.

"Most people inherit the symbols they use from the world around them. We in the church already have a rich language of symbols to draw upon. Probably the most obvious is the cross. Its simplicity provides a powerful focus. With it we can focus our will, use it as a shield or as a weapon.

"For you it makes more sense for you to create your own symbols. They're just a tool to help refine your ability. You have no shared history to gain any benefit from established symbols. So use what feels right for you. Allow your will to shape the symbol and symbol will then focus your will."

I let that sink in and thought about the rocks in all of their heads. I wondered what would happen if those rocks broke.

Chapter 34
The joy of shields

As I lay on the narrow bed in the darkness I thought about what I learned over the past few weeks. It never occurred to me before to use abstract symbols as a means to focus the effect of my abilities. The other advantage I learnt was that they provided convenient shorthand. With them I could compile an arsenal of effects that would be available at any moment. I thought of all the impulses I pushed into people's minds over the years and how much easier it would have been to re-use common symbols.

In a strange way it felt satisfying to learn something new. I'd wielded power before, but to add some finesse to it was a pleasant feeling. The fact that it also made me more capable was no bad thing either. Each day I felt myself becoming more capable. The thought of a rematch with Lazarus remained prominent in my mind. I didn't fool myself into thinking I'd beat him a fair fight, but an unfair one would do. My revenge didn't need to be tainted with honour or any of that crap.

Despite the headache I slept soundly that night. I awoke feeling refreshed and eager to learn more. It occurred to me that I hadn't dreamed since I had been brought here. I wondered if that was intentional or not.

When breakfast concluded Friar Francis introduced the day's new topic. "Continuing on from your extra-curricular activities we're going to look at shields today."

So they had observed what I did in the evenings. I doubted that they used technology to monitor my activities. That meant they must either be able to sense a presence inside their barrier or they were aware when I made changes to their barriers. I'd bet on the second option, but either way I deemed it useful information.

"We'll start with forming a personal shield. At its most basic a shield protects you from attack or external influence. With novices we start with having them visualize a shield as a bright blue aura around them. It's a good place to start, so why don't you give it a try?"

Simple enough I thought, and coated myself in a bright blue aura as requested.

"In your case it's more of a beacon than a shield. It would protect you well enough, but would also attract attention for miles around. Make the aura thinner, so it follows the contours of your body."

I toned it down a bit.

"Good. Now, the strength of a shield isn't determined by its thickness, but in its density. If you remember the exercises where you penetrated various barriers, it was the density that forced you to use ever smaller probes. The denser the shield, the tighter the energy is packed so the smaller the imperfections. That makes it harder to penetrate. Your power or strength of will and mastery of the technique is what determines how strong a shield you can create."

That made sense. I refocused the aura, making it thinner still while also forcing more will into the smaller volume.

"Excellent. Now we can look at increasing the complexity of the barrier. The easiest way to do this is to create multiple shields, each one layered on top of the other."

I saw a problem with this. "If they can penetrate one then surely penetrating the others is no more difficult?"

"That's a fair point. You're jumping the gun a bit, but I expected no less from you."

That fucking smile again.

"To make the different layers more effective you should move the layers. That will cost them time, giving you more time to react. You have to shift the layers at different speeds which makes it more difficult to probe. To stop an attack the shield must be stronger than your opponent. In essence that means that the imperfections he seeks must be smaller than he can focus his will. Having to do this across multiple layers will compound the challenge."

I gave this a try.

"Ok, that's good. Now instead of layering them, try entwining them so the layers pass through each other. Think of it like tying it into a knot. The more complex the knot, the more effective it will be."

Again I did as he bid.

"That's good. Now I'll try breaking the shield."

I sensed his probes immediately. He attacked from multiple directions at once with countless tiny barbs. They flickered across my shield as they hunted for weaknesses. At first I reacted to each probe, strengthened the shield where he probed.

"Good. You respond quickly, but keep your awareness loose, and don't restrict your focus so much." He then increased the number of probes and I attempted to match him. As he no doubt intended. Of course it was a mistake.

When I responded to one attack he swiftly switched and I fell into a cycle of responding.

"Don't allow yourself to be overwhelmed. Even a weak opponent can create countless probes. You cannot track each one."

He was correct. I tried to track too many things and the first of his probes broke through. I switched tactics and collapsed the penetrated shields then added new ones beneath those.

"Excellent," I heard him say. I hoped this strained him as much as it did me. Sweat beaded on my brow as I struggled to concentrate.

The Friar changed his tactics as well. This time instead of probing he focused his will into a single lance that slammed into the shield. The tip was surprisingly soft and splashed against the shield. It split into billions of filaments that filled the imperfections in my shields. As clusters found the gaps they instantly burst, shattering new holes.

I thought of a new method of attack and instead of resisting I allowed the filaments to penetrate and then swallowed them with new shields thus trapping them. I then pulled at them drawing them into the pockets I created. His attack weakened as he found himself being dragged in to these pockets.

"Enough." He panted. "That was well done. The point as I'm sure you've realised is that your defence must be dynamic. For the untrained it is often just a clash of wills. The problem with that is if you pour all your strength and focus into a single move, you'll often end up outmanoeuvred."

With a chuckle he continued. "In many ways it's like fighting a boxing match and playing chess at the same time. Agility can often beat power, and keeping moves in reserve can change the balance of a contest. The other problem with putting all your will into a single attack is that you don't know if the other person is the same, or if you are actually battling more than one person.

"And as you've just demonstrated, offence can often be the best form of defence."

I couldn't disagree with that. In my experience a good defence is about waiting to unleash a brutal offence.

We continued with more exercises until Hammond brought in a selection of sandwiches for lunch. As usual, the Friar left me alone to eat. When I finished he quickly returned and resumed the lesson.

"At the start I told you to create an aura of blue. We always start with blue as it is a strong colour, well suited for defence. It's also an easy way to encourage putting a lot of energy in a smaller volume. Like with stars, the brightest stars tend to be blue and are also smaller than the red ones.

"For more experienced initiates colour can be used to add complexity to your shields. Colours can be given meanings, essentially treating them as another symbol, or as a way of flavouring symbols. If you are juggling different effects at the same time, they provide a quick mechanism for keeping track of them.

"This leads me to the final lesson for today. A shield itself is a form of symbol, but it can work the other way round. If you create a symbol — let's say — that is a snare, similar to how you trapped my probes earlier, you can take that symbol and entwine it into your shield layers. Another way to look at it is to take the symbol and stretch it over your shield. And of course, with an array of symbols you can easily layer multiple effects.

"That's a good way to add traps or triggers to your shields. Let's try it now. Create a symbol in your mind — keep it simple for now. Create a symbol that sparks when another presence touches it."

I shaped the Snap Dragon symbol in my mind.

"Now raise a shield. Keep it simple just a single layer. Now merge the symbol with the shield."

I thought of a better way. The Snap Dragon symbol now formed a layer that acted as a shield but sparked when something touched it. I told the Friar that I was ready and I watched the shield sparkle as he probed at it. I changed the symbol again, wearing a small grin of my own. The sparkles now buzzed around him like bees.

"All right, I see you've learnt how to modify your symbols on the fly. That will come in useful. Now for your next exercise ..."

A knock at the door interrupted him. That was unusual — we were never disturbed. He opened the door, and I heard a muffled conversation. I expanded my awareness to try and listen in. The Friar glanced at me, then stepped out of the room. When he closed the door it blocked me off.

Fair enough. I looked at Hammond standing by the door, impassive. I didn't enter his mind, although I still sensed the rock within him. It suddenly struck me. The rock formed a special type of shield, a shield on the inside. A shield on the inside is not easily noticed. It provides a hidden last line of defence. Very clever.

The Friar interrupted my thoughts as he walked back into the room. He nodded at Hammond before saying. "One of our teams has spotted Lazarus. We fly out in an hour. Hammond will help you get ready."

Chapter 35
To sunny climes

As Hammond locked me back in my cell, I listened to the sounds of hurried activity down the hall. He returned a few minutes later carrying a bundle of fresh clothes for me to wear. He instructed me to get changed quickly. I dressed all in black: black combat trousers, black T-shirt, black boots, even black underwear. I looked like a modern day ninja.

After I dressed, he then told me to lie down. He held a syringe in his hand.

"So I don't get to enjoy the ride then?" I asked him.

"Not this time," He replied before expertly injecting the solution into my arm.

This seems a little unfair I thought as I slipped into the warm darkness.

* * *

Once again I had no idea how long it had been when I awoke. Hunger rumbled in my stomach so it must have been many hours. I groaned from the stiffness in my muscles. Maybe it was longer than I first thought. I looked around. I was in a room, not a cell. The bed underneath me had a proper mattress, and there was even real furniture: a dresser, a wardrobe. Nothing fancy; in fact, they looked quite rustic. It seemed that I was going up in the world. There was even a real window, framed with flowery curtains. Despite the hunger pangs, I considered this one of my better wake-ups in recent history.

I expanded my awareness to look further into my surroundings. I encountered no barrier on the walls around the room. I sensed some form of shielding a few hundred yards away around the whole building, but nothing restricted my ability.

The temptation to soar was great, but I thought there was no point upsetting the management just yet.

Standing up I suddenly realised how warm it was. I moved over to the window and opened it. The air outside felt even warmer, although the movement of the breeze was pleasant upon my skin. I looked out through the window. It looked like we were in a Mediterranean farmhouse. In front of me I saw a guard standing by the gateway cut in a rough stone wall. He scanned all around and noticed me with an offhand salute.

I waved back. It only seemed polite.

Farmland surrounded the house. In my view was a field of parched wheat and another of scrubby grass where goats and sheep chewed lazily in the warm sun. This was easily the best view I'd seen in quite some time. In the distance stood a range of hills. I noticed something strange: giant flags had been cut into the soil of the hills. I remembered somebody telling me about this. It meant that we were in Cyprus.

The door opened and I heard the sound of a normal latch, not a lock. Hammond poked his head through. "Ah good, you're awake. Follow me. The Friar is about to begin the briefing."

He led me down the narrow stairs, past a kitchen that smelled divine. My stomach growled in protest as I walked by. We continued along the corridor and into an annex. The stonework here appeared to be newer. This section must have been built after the main farmhouse.

The Friar stood beside the large screen fixed to the far wall of the room. Six other people waited with him, all sitting on cheap plastic chairs. Half of them wore black paramilitary gear, similar to my clothing. The others dressed in cassocks like the Friar. I picked an empty chair to one side of the room. The Friar nodded a greeting at me, which I casually returned. Some of the other faces looked at me with curiosity. Hammond pulled a chair up behind me, making sure to position himself between me and the door.

"I'll start from the top for the benefit of the newcomers," the Friar said as the screen snapped to life displaying a map. He pointed at it. "Here, high up in the hills is the old Crusader Fort, in ruins now. It was built in the late Thirteenth Century on the site of an ancient Christian church, itself just a ruin at the time."

The map dissolved into a picture of a ruined fortress perched precariously on top of a cliff. "Here is one of the locations for the events that Lazarus must complete." The image switched back to the map. "There is only one road to the ruin." He traced the route through the hills, stopped at a small area below the fort. "Here is the nearest village — well, more of a hamlet really. There's a dozen houses and a single cafe where the road forks. One road leads north, to the fort. The other follows this line of hills to the east."

The image changed. This time the screen showed a balding middle-aged man. His skin looked reddened by the sun, his paunch clearly visible beneath his stretched shirt. "A week ago this man was spotted by our surveillance team entering the village. He booked the only room in the cafe and has stayed there since. So far he has been observed wandering around the hills, concentrating mostly around the ruins."

"We've identified him as Sam Jenkins. Twenty years ago he was a well known Evangelist preacher, who then disappeared. He's been tracked since then in Europe, Africa and occasionally in the US. On many of those occasions he has been seen in the company of known associates of Lazarus. We believe he's a money and PR man. He helps set up new contacts and funnels funds wherever needed for Lazarus' network.

"He is definitely not a field operative and we think that he's acting as a scout here for Lazarus himself. Which indicates that Lazarus is really having to scrape the barrel if he has to use somebody like Mr Jenkins in the field."

This time the screen displayed a satellite image of the village, the cafe highlighted. "Yesterday our friends in the British listening post on one of their airbases here in Cyprus intercepted a call from a mobile phone in the cafe. The parties on the call where identified by voice analysis as Sam Jenkins and Lazarus himself. The contents of the call indicate that in two days' time Lazarus will meet Mr Jenkins at the cafe. The meeting is supposed to happen at midday. Their plans after that time are unknown.

"We have people at all of the airports as well as the smaller airfields watching for Lazarus' arrival. We also have all of the ports watched, but this coast has too many small fishing villages so there are a number of places where he could sneak in undetected.

"You all know who we face and the challenge that he presents. We've brought in a new member of the team who will be able to help us." With this he indicated me, and everyone swivelled in their chairs to get a better look. They knew I was not one of them. I was an outsider and that was enough to make them curious.

"We've positioned an observation team at the ruins and another watching the village. The village team are watching from a distance, which is far from ideal, but we want to avoid alerting Mr Jenkins."

He paused again while the screen changed. This time it showed a blurred image of a man in his mid-thirties. He had an intense look about on his face, with dark, shadowed eyes. I recognised him immediately.

"This is our target, Lazarus. You all know what he is and the danger he represents. As I mentioned in the earlier briefings he's close to achieving his goals. Much too close for our, or anyone else's comfort. We have to take this opportunity to ensure that we take Lazarus down for good.

"Your first task is to familiarise yourselves with the local terrain. You'll have to do that remotely via simulation for now. We will reconvene in a couple of hours to go through the plan."

The Friar then stepped away and headed towards me. I sensed Hammond standing up, so I did the same. The others crowded around the laptops. Two of the military looking guys left the room.

"You should get something to eat." The Friar's suggestion sounded good to me. "I also want you to mask the perimeter guards. I doubt that Lazarus' people have the time or the manpower to scout this far out, but if they do I don't want to make it easy for them. Go to the kitchens — they will sort you out. Hammond, you stay with him and make sure you are both back for the planning session in two hours."

I expanded my awareness beyond the farmhouse to get a feel for the immediate area. I sensed the three guards on the perimeter wall and masked them from view. The other guards watched from vantage points in the farmhouse itself — I did the same with them and faded their presence from sight. Anyone attempting to view remotely wouldn't see anything interesting. I headed to the kitchen, following the delightfully enticing smell all the way. Hammond, my ever present guard dog, followed in my wake.

I ate so much that I needed to rest for an hour before I could move again. I liked it inside the kitchen. The smell was delicious and homely. I hadn't experienced anything like that since my childhood. We sat at the scarred wooden table and tucked into the array of different dishes. Hammond sat opposite me. He didn't seem interested in conversation.

The food tasted amazing. I couldn't identify most of it, but everything was freshly cooked and divine to eat. I washed it down with iced tea, something I had never drunk before. I found it very refreshing. As I recovered from this feast, I sat and expanded my awareness again. I didn't enter anybody's mind. I just brushed past them to get a sense for who I now worked with.

Every single one of them held a rock in their heads. Some were smaller than others, but I detected that anchor in all of them. The clergy all shielded their minds. Some were strong, but none quite as strong as Friar Francis.

I relaxed back in the chair. I felt content and snoozed for a while before Hammond touched my arm and told me that it was time to go.

Chapter 36
The best laid plans

The planning group consisted of the same people from the earlier briefing. Everyone was already sat except for Friar Francis when I arrived with Hammond. As before the Friar stood by the screen. This time it displayed a high resolution image of the village. I positioned myself to the side of the room. Hammond sat close behind and we all listened as the Friar began talking.

"Before we start I've just been informed that a deal has been reached with the Turkish security forces. They will turn a blind eye for the next few days in this area of operations. They've been told that there is a combined UK and US anti-terrorist operation. They're not happy about not being involved, especially as it is on their soil, but in return there'll only be minimal objections to some of their operations in northern Iraq. At least we won't have to worry too much about the Turkish army turning up unannounced."

A few relieved nods from the military looking personnel.

"Before we outline the plan, let's recap the two things we know for certain — or at least as certain as we can be."

More nods and a few wry smiles that time.

"The first is the where. We know that the meeting will take place at the cafe. The second is the when. We know that the meeting will take place at midday in two days' time.

"The objective of the mission is to take Lazarus down for good. We can't achieve this through conventional means, so we need to get, hmm, let's call him 'Mr X' for now ..." At this he points at me. 'Mr X,' I liked it, very mysterious. I thought about having it printed on my luggage. "We need to get 'Mr X' in close proximity to Lazarus."

"How close?" asked the military looking man sat at the front of the room. His accent sounded German, or maybe Austrian or Swiss.

"As close as we are right now. He will need to be within touching distance of Lazarus."

A few muffled curses from around the room.

"This farm is the current staging area. We are two miles from the target zone. On the local roads that's about fifteen minutes travel. As soon as we receive confirmation Lazarus is at the cafe, the snatch team will leave here and approach the target at speed. The village observation team will also move to block any vehicle trying to escape the village from the other access road. The team at the fort will do the same."

I could see this wasn't a popular plan.

"So the target is going to hear us coming and may have several minutes to escape?" asked the German sounding soldier.

"We will have all the access routes covered, and if he tries to escape cross country the observation team will have him in view for at least five miles in every direction. Unless he heads north into the hills, in which case he will run into the team from the fort."

"What are the chances that Lazarus will arrive alone?" Another good question from our Germanic friend.

"We expect he'll have at least a couple of bodyguards. They'll be capable, but not the same level of threat that Lazarus himself poses. It's likely that there will be a fire fight when we snatch him. We don't need them alive and if Lazarus himself was that easy to kill then we wouldn't have this problem. Which means we can go in noisy and hard. I want everyone to watch their targets — dead locals won't go down well, but the target is the priority, no matter what the cost.

"It's far from ideal, I'd prefer that we staged closer so he has hardly any warning before we move in."

"So why don't we?" I asked.

"Lazarus has a gift that rivals yours, 'Mr X', so he will probe the area as he moves in, and if he detects anything suspicious at all then he won't walk into the trap. We estimate that we need to be at least a mile away for our presence not to be detected. That estimate does take into account the brothers here capable of shielding.

"Once we have Lazarus, we bring him back here and, with your assistance, we finish the job."

"I can hide us," I said confidently. "If we stage the night before, nearer to the cafe, I can maintain the illusion and hide us. When the time comes we won't have to drive for fifteen minutes to get in range."

I saw that there were Doubting Thomases everywhere in the room.

"I can do this. Even if he does get close and smells a rat we'll be closer in to chase him."

Another soldier spoke, he definitely wasn't a believer. As he began to protest I expanded my awareness and made Hammond disappear. The soldier didn't realise at first what I had done — when he realised I heard him mutter. It sounded French. Maybe he was Swiss as well?

It put a smile on the Friar's and Hammond's faces at any rate.

The Friar thought for a minute then nodded. "Ok. When Lazarus arrives we hit them hard, use stun grenades to buy us a few seconds to take down the guards. With Lazarus himself we use tazers and then dope him up to keep him quiet for the journey back."

I raised my hand, playing the shy schoolboy. "Might I suggest pumping him full of some LSD or something similar as well. It might make things a bit easier for me when I have to go in."

"I think we can arrange that." He then motioned at one of the other priests, who quickly left the room.

I contemplated for a moment. Something nagged at me. One of Hammond's memories surfaced from when I delved into his past, and the memory brought with it an idea. "Is there a sniper with the observation team?"

"Yes, they'll provide long distance cover and help block that access road."

"Can they cover the village?"

"It's well over a mile. They might be able to help with larger targets like vehicles, but close support would be extremely difficult at that range."

"Didn't Officer Hammond here take a Taliban down at over a mile in Afghanistan? Record shot for a Royal Marine and all that?"

There's some impressed looks from the other soldier boys in the room. Hammond nodded casually as if this was an everyday occurrence.

"So put him with the observation team with one of those big bastard sniper rifles. You know the ones that will put a hole in an engine block at over a mile. Then as soon as Lazarus sits down, BOOM, headshot."

The Friar wasn't convinced. "That won't kill him."

"I know it won't, but it'll give him the mother of all headaches and I'm willing to bet that it will slow him down enough to zap him unconscious and then fill him with drugs."

His expression indicated that he was wavering. "It might work. One of the .50 calibres would also be good for stopping any vehicles trying to escape." I knew the other part that worried him. He was relying on Hammond to be my keeper. The same thought had already occurred to me. Now he'd have to do that himself. We needed to take Lazarus down quickly to stand any chance of success. My window of opportunity widened slightly.

I felt the others in the team siding with me on this. Their mood lightened. With something resembling a working plan, they could see a faint glimmer of light at the end of the tunnel.

"And to help finish him I suggest that we just keep pumping him with drugs all the way back. The more stressed his brain and body are, the easier he will be for me to deal with. After all, I do have some experience with delving into fucked up minds."

Friar Francis finally relented. "Ok, we'll do it your way. Tomorrow night the snatch team will drive into the village. We'll need to find somewhere to park where people won't accidently bump into the van. We sit and wait for Lazarus to show up for the meeting. As soon as his presence is confirmed we approach the cafe as Hammond shoots him. We then mop up any bodyguards, dose and taze him and put him in the van.

"Just make sure you are ready to do your part. And remember I will be with you every step of the way. And don't forget our insurance."

I took that as a compliment. I experienced a thrill of excitement. I'd never really planned things out like this before, it was quite a novelty. I thought I now had a reasonable chance of achieving my revenge.

It's the bit afterwards I needed to plan for now.

Chapter 37
Testing times

I enjoyed a longer sleep than everybody else. The noises of the farm and the warm sunshine through the window provided a gentle and not-unpleasant wake-up call. As I leisurely allowed my senses to return I listened to the bustle of activity downstairs. It was still early in the day. Through the window, the sun sat low against the horizon. I guessed they were happy to have me out of the way for now. I was on the team, but not part of it. That was fine with me, but it cut both ways.

While I showered and dressed I contemplated the upcoming action. I'd agreed to do it and I knew from my previous encounter that it wouldn't be easy. As powerful as Lazarus seemed, I expected that once the bullets and the drugs put him down, entering his mind would be simple. I looked forward to some payback.

The big question yet to be answered was: what next? The Friar had already made it clear that freedom wouldn't be an option. Now was probably the best opportunity to escape that I would get. So, why stay? Why didn't I take advantage of their focus being elsewhere and run for it? They had the tracker and the collar, but they also had other concerns. Lazarus was clearly a big deal for them, a bigger and more immediate threat than me. Would they call off the attack to hunt me down? They had other resources I'm sure and no doubt Interpol would be on the case, but I would have a head start.

The tracker they implanted was a concern. I knew that it was real, without it the Friar and Hammond couldn't have rescued me. I could handle the tracker. I just had to find the right people quickly enough. There was no question of whether they'd do what I wanted or not.

I owed them for the rescue. More importantly I also owed Lazarus some pain. It reduced my chances of an easy escape by sticking with the plan, but I would pay what I owed. Afterwards there would be an opportunity.

Tantalising scents from the kitchen enticed me downstairs. Along the way I bumped into one of soldiers smoking by the back door. He generously gave me a cigarette and lit it for me. We didn't talk. We were just two strangers standing together on foreign soil enjoying the morning sun and a quick smoke.

The breakfast arrayed on the table in the kitchen wasn't one I would have recognised, but the varied selection of meats, cheeses and fresh warm bread more than compensated for its unfamiliarity. Uncomplicated fare that tasted amazing. A glass of creamy milk contrasted with the bitter coffee that washed down this goodness. I'm not usually a coffee man, but I discovered why people drank it. It certainly picks you up in the morning.

Hammond and the Friar found me lazing in the kitchen, finishing the thick coffee. "We're going for a little trip," Hammond told me so I followed them out into the yard. As we passed through the house I heard grumbling from the various soldier types. I expanded my awareness so I could hear their complaints more clearly.

The principal complaint came from the lack of preparation time they had to work with. They had nowhere to rehearse the assault properly, instead having to rely on paper and virtual reality scenarios to learn the terrain. Exposed as they were in this farmhouse they couldn't even practice their contact drills. I didn't know what a contact drill was, but it sounded important.

Their second major complaint was, of course, me. I got the feeling that they weren't happy dealing with new people at all. Especially when that new person appeared to be a creepy individual with mystic powers. I resisted the temptation to improve their feelings towards me.

We climbed into an old Land Rover. Battered and dusty, it was clearly a veteran of these parts. Another monk already sat in the driver's seat. When the doors closed he revved the engine and drove down the bumpy track.

Hammond loomed in the seat beside me. The Friar sat in the passenger seat up front. He turned and raised his voice to be heard above the engine noise, then said, "I think you've bitten off more than you can chew. Today you have to prove to me that you are capable of cloaking us from Lazarus tomorrow. You can start right now. Make this vehicle invisible to anyone who can see us."

I relaxed, expanded my awareness, and then fixed the picture in my mind, with the jeep removed.

"Don't be a smart-ass," growled Hammond. "Everyone in the vehicle needs to be invisible as well!"

I offered a little smile. I thought it a pity there was nobody around to witness the four people floating down the road. I corrected the image and maintained my focus. Before we reached the coast road we were invisible to anyone around.

Now I had never experienced driving where the other passengers couldn't see you. It made for an interesting experience and I tipped a metaphorical hat to our driver who clearly possessed nerves of steel. Luckily for us the road remained fairly empty and we didn't encounter many other vehicles, but we did have a few near misses.

Junctions proved the biggest danger. Drivers approached the junction and not seeing anything else coming pulled out. Of course they weren't to know that we were in front of them. I think our driver spent most of the journey cursing in Italian. It could have been Latin. I didn't really know the difference.

In one respect the Friar was quite correct. I had underestimated how difficult it was. The first problem I encountered was that we moved quickly and at first I wasn't compensating for that. We reached the edge of the mental picture I formed and flickered back into view. I quickly changed the picture so it updated as we moved. Soon I was able leave it as a background task, let it tick away at the back of my mind.

The other issue proved to be one of scale. The road ran along the line of hills, about half way up the slopes. It twisted and wound through the hills so that sometimes we could see for miles, and at other times only the corner ahead. I learned that pushing my awareness higher above the scene helped alleviate this problem.

I knew that the actual task of hiding the vehicle and snatch team from Lazarus wouldn't be as complicated as this. That provided me with some small relief. We would be in a stationary vehicle and physically hidden out of the way, but it was good practice and my arrogance turned to confidence in the task ahead, rather than the simple arrogance from the previous day's briefing. Annoying as it felt, the Friar had been right.

As we drove, Hammond and the Friar maintained a constant conversation with me. I realised what they were doing. They attempted to distract me with a barrage of trivial questions about my past, was I into football, nonsense stuff. They continuously switched subjects so I had to think about the answers for their questions.

We continued to drive for about an hour before turning off the coast road and onto another rough track that twisted up the hill. At the top of the hill we encountered a small monastery. It looked old, the stonework pocked and bleached by the sun. It was a squat building, dominated by a large stone cross and enclosed with a high stone wall. We pulled into the driveway, the tyres crunching on the loose gravel. A monk tending some plants by the entrance turned in surprise, his shock apparent as the car shimmered into view.

Friar Francis appeared pleased with this response. He clambered out of the car and said, "This isn't a Dominican monastery, but the brothers here are known for their mystic pursuits. I have already spoken to the head of their order and they're going to help test your cloak of this vehicle."

With that he walked up to the lone monk and, after a brief conversation, they entered the gateway. While they were gone we moved the car and parked it at the far side of the entrance. Hammond jumped out and swept the wheel marks from the gravel with a large piece of bush. I then resumed the mental picture and erased us from view.

For the rest of the day I maintained the cloak. It took a lot of effort, but I managed without any major mishap. Different monks wandered out of the entrance and looked around the driveway. I sensed probes lancing through my illusion. I ignored them, allowed them to pass through the cloak unhindered. I knew that it if I resisted the probes that would give me away. They were already inside the effect, so could discern no change.

As I had on the trip here I maintained the cloak over a wide area. A good job too, because a prickling in my awareness led me to an observer on a hill across the valley. With my mind's eye I saw one of the guards from the farmhouse observing the monastery through powerful binoculars.

That Friar Francis was a sly one. Luckily he was well within the zone of my awareness.

All day I kept it up, although I really wished we had brought some food and water with us. I asked Hammond if that was deliberate, but he just grinned at me. He'd seen more than his fair share of days in the hot sun in dusty lands so it didn't bother him too much. I mentally shrugged and remain focused on the task in hand.

Finally as dusk began to settle the Friar returned. I thought every monk from the monastery now stood by the gate. The Friar instructed me to turn off the cloak and we rippled into view before the assembled brothers. We saw a few surprised faces and a couple of restrained nods, but the Friar seemed pleased as he told the driver to return home. As the sky darkened, he deemed it wise to drive back to the farmhouse visible to the other road users.

It appeared that I had passed his test. I know I shouldn't have, but I did experience a little spark of pride.

Once we arrived back at the farmhouse Hammond told me to get a few hours' rest, since we would be moving out at midnight. So, I ignored the bustle of the soldiers preparing equipment and checking their weapons and headed to the small bedroom and lay down to rest.

Chapter 38
Going in hard

It was still dark when Hammond roused me from my brief slumber. I'd managed to get a couple of hours' rest and felt better for it. I quickly dressed in the clean black fatigues, shirt and boots that he threw on the bed. I manoeuvred the shock collar over the shirt to prevent chafing. Naturally I wasn't given a weapon of any kind, but I did receive an assault vest with a water pack built in. It weighed heavy upon my shoulders. I investigated the various pockets and discovered a variety of energy bars and an assortment of gadgets.

Within minutes we all assembled in the courtyard of the farmhouse. The moon sat high in the sky, but looked thin and cast very little light. I took a moment to gaze upwards — it looked simply magnificent. I had never seen a sky so clear before, the stars hardly twinkling at all. I never realised how full the night sky was. I could have stared at it for hours, lost in its infinite majesty.

One of the soldiers interrupted my contemplation by handing me a pair of night vision goggles. Wearing the goggles the world transformed into black and shades of luminous green. I found the view confusing and removed them. My awareness enabled me to see much more clearly than the goggles.

We all bundled into the van. It felt a little too cosy in the back with the four soldiers of the snatch team, Friar Francis, Hammond and I. I checked my watch, another present from the grim faced soldier. I saw that it was soon after midnight when we left the farm and headed onto the road towards the village.

As we approached the village the van stopped. The driver switched off the headlights and put on his night vision goggles. Hammond moved to get out of the van — he now had to tab the few miles around the village to join up with the observation team. He needed to be in position before dawn broke.

Tab meant walking very quickly while carrying a load of crap, apparently.

He collected his gear which included the biggest gun I had ever seen. Before he climbed out through the side door he clapped me on the shoulder and wished me good luck. I was a bit taken aback by this gesture and could only nod back in acknowledgement.

With Hammond gone into the night the van seemed much more spacious. Friar Francis said to me in a low voice, "Time to do your thing. Just do what you did yesterday, keep us hidden until Lazarus arrives and the first shot is fired."

"Ok." As I had all through the previous day I expanded my awareness and erased the van and its remaining occupants from view. "Done," I told him. He then instructed the driver to carry on. The driver kept the headlights off and navigated using his night vision goggles. We travelled slowly, minimizing noise as much as possible.

While I practised throughout the previous day, the snatch team had been busy locating suitable hiding places. They found a ruined barn on the outskirts of the village, only a few hundred yards from the cafe. Once Lazarus' arrival had been confirmed the snatch team would approach the cafe from the rear. They'd then launch a surprise assault on Lazarus and any companions he had with him. I would have to mask the four soldiers as they approached as well as maintaining the cloak over the van and the rest of us.

We crept slowly through the village. As we passed by the first group of houses a dog barked, shattering the still quiet of the night. I cast a soothing thought at it which calmed the beast. The driver carefully reversed us into the ruined building and switched off the engine.

Other than the sounds of our breathing, there was absolute silence in the van. The time now read after two am. In four hours' time dawn would break. The Friar and the snatch team each brought laptops which they now opened. The soldier sat in the passenger seat quietly snuck out of the van and set up a small satellite antenna. Once connected to the laptops their screens bloomed into life. Each now displayed various images of the sleeping village. All appeared grainy from the light intensification filters.

I couldn't nap to pass the time — I was too wired. Waiting for events to unfold was never my style. Planning and waiting still felt alien to me. Every so often I heard one of the soldiers talking to the observation team, their voices little more than a soft murmur. I still couldn't quite place their accents. They all sounded German or French.

"They're Swiss Guards," The Friar told me after I gave in and asked. "They are a special team from the Swiss Guards that has protected the Vatican for hundreds of years. You don't need to worry. They know what they're doing."

I wasn't worried. I felt insulted by the suggestion.

The time passed slowly. I daren't use my awareness to satisfy my curiosity and investigate the few houses. Any slip up would betray our position and all the effort so far would be wasted. I wanted my showdown, so I kept my inquisitive urges in check.

Dawn finally arrived unannounced. We all suddenly realised the sky had started to lighten. A radio report informed us that Hammond had arrived at the observation team and that he was now setting up in the camouflaged hide they had built.

On the screens we watched the village slowly come to life. Most of the locals were elderly. We saw a few of the younger residents leaving in old cars presumably to work in the town further down the valley. The cafe opened and a few locals walked there for their morning coffee and, for one bent old man, his breakfast.

The sky was unmarred by clouds and as the sun rose so did the temperature. The back of the van quickly became hot and stuffy. I took a drink from the camel pack on my back, surprised to find it was still cool. I wondered how much water it contained.

We opened the doors and windows to allow the air to circulate. There was little breeze and the air remained hot and oppressive. The Friar and the soldiers took it in their stride. I sweated buckets and struggled to breathe. Noticing my discomfort, the Friar advised me to relax.

Relax, he said! It was a million fucking degrees in that van! I smiled as that reminded me of an old joke. The Friar was right, I must relax. I retreated a little inside myself and injected calm into my own mind. With great focus I pushed the right connections, my body wasn't any cooler, but it wasn't stressing as much about it. It helped a little.

As the morning dragged by, the pace of the village, already sedate, slowed even further. At eleven o'clock Sam Jenkins made his appearance. He sat at one of the tables in the shade of the building. The cafe owner brought him iced tea and he drank it slowly. Although he held a local newspaper in his hand, he spent most of the time carefully watching the road. An oversized mobile phone rested on the table in front of him.

Half an hour later a vehicle was seen heading towards the village. The observation team reported that it was a police car, two officers visible inside.

This caused some consternation between the Friar and the snatch team. The area was supposed to be clear of the local security forces. The Friar attempted to calm their fears — the local police wouldn't have been told, otherwise word would have leaked. This was probably just a local patrol that would soon move on and there would be nothing to worry about.

No-one appeared convinced. Lazarus was due to arrive in less than half an hour's time.

The police parked next to the cafe, exited their car and, after a quick and polite greeting to Jenkins, sat at the table farthest away from him.

We watched the cafe closely on the laptop screens. The visual feed wasn't real time video, only static images that updated every second or two, so it was like watching a slide show. The images appeared crystal clear, every detail visible.

Midday passed slowly. It remained baking hot in the van — even the soldiers now showed some signs of discomfort. The Friar alone remained unruffled. The two police officers ordered a second cup of coffee. They seemed to be in no hurry to leave.

Another half hour crawled by and Jenkins answered a phone call. We saw him talking, but covered his mouth so the lip reading software had nothing to follow. He glanced briefly at the chatting officers and then the call ended. Jenkins called for the owner and held a brief conversation with him.

"Could the police be providing additional security?" one of the soldiers asked. "They're probably just having a quiet one out of the way," another replied. "So what do we do if they're still here and Lazarus arrives?" the first one asked.

"We proceed with the plan," the Friar ordered. "If possible use a non-lethal takedown, but the mission objective remains the same. Lazarus is the priority."

On the screen we observed Jenkins receive another call. It lasted only thirty seconds. A few minutes later the owner brought out a number of dishes, placed them on the table before going to the policeman. Their conversation looked lively. They appeared to know each other well.

The tension in the van was palpable. By now Lazarus was two hours late. Was he holding off because the police were here?

Fifteen minutes later the policemen both stood and, after waving to the cafe owner, walked towards their car. Filled with nervous anticipation we watched them on the stuttering screen as they climbed in and drove away. I could almost hear the sighs of relief from everyone around me.

As they drove down the road the observation team called in, they spotted a black SUV heading up the road towards the village. On our screens we watched the black car moving closer. They passed by the police car without incident. The observation team failed to identify anyone in the SUV. All they reported was a driver and somebody else sitting beside them. The darkened rear windows prevented them from seeing if there was anybody else inside.

At the same time I shuddered as a ripple passed through my awareness.

The shiver felt as if someone had just walked over my grave. I maintained the mental picture and suppressed my mounting excitement.

The SUV stopped in front of the cafe, the engine still running as the passenger stepped out. We watched frames of a brief conversation between him and Jenkins. The cafe owner went into the building. I bet it was lovely and cool in there. I sipped some more water and tried to ignore the sweat pouring from my brow.

One of the rear doors opened. A man in a light linen suit climbed out. The build looked about right, but he didn't face the camera so we couldn't confirm his identity. The driver also got out and followed the man in the suit. Both driver and passenger were dressed smartly in trousers and shirts. They both wore jackets despite the blazing sun.

The driver waited by the SUV while the other stood in the shade of the cafe, near to the suited man. The suited man sat at the same table as Jenkins, and as he twisted his body into the chair his face came into view.

"Target confirmed." I heard the tension in the Friar's voice. "Let's move."

The soldiers in the snatch team deployed from the van quietly, and followed the contours of the houses as they approached the cafe from the rear. In my mental picture they did not exist.

The snatch team split into two, each pair stealthily flanking the cafe. "Take the shot." I heard the Friar order. A single clap of thunder reverberated between the hills. On the screen in one image Lazarus could be seen talking to

Jenkins, in the next he was on the ground, the table and chairs captured in mid fall.

The snatch team lobbed their stun grenades around the cafe. They exploded, the burst of bright light distorting several images in a row. Another boom echoed across the landscape. When the screens cleared the guard by the SUV was down, the front wing of the SUV splashed with dark, lumpy liquid. Jenkins was also down. In the next frame I saw one of the soldiers take aim. A moment later we heard that nearer gunshot. His partner now knelt by Lazarus' body.

I couldn't believe it — in those few frames he had moved.

Our driver now drove the van towards the cafe. We would be there in seconds. I kept watching the screen. The other pair of the snatch team both shot the other guard, who fell across one of the tables. His hand never reached the pistol in a shoulder holster beneath his jacket. I now heard the rattle of automatic gunfire.

The van screeched to a halt in front of the cafe, only just missing the SUV. The soldiers dragged Lazarus' body towards the van. I saw the gaping hole in his chest. The dirt of the ground was visible through the meaty hole. I saw his fingers moving.

The observation team reported over the radio that the police car had stopped and was turning round. A third clap of thunder and the team reported vehicle neutralised and the officers cowering behind their car.

Lazarus was now being dragged into the van. The Friar swiftly injected him with the drug cocktail prepared earlier. As the soldiers climbed in, he took another syringe and injected that as well. The side door slammed shut as the van sped down the road.

Chapter 39
The journey

During the return journey, I took the time to examine Lazarus lying unconscious on the floor of the van. He didn't look so remarkable now. The face appeared the same as when I had last met him, except for the flecks of blood matting his beard. I wanted to dive straight into his head, but forced myself to stick with the plan. I consoled myself with a kick at his head. The Friar chastised me with a small frown.

Inevitably I found my gaze drawn to the gaping hole in his chest. Even in gloom of the van I saw the flesh knitting itself slowly back together. If I needed any further convincing of his power there it was.

As agreed in the plan, we injected him with a cocktail of drugs. Most were from the Friar to keep him unconscious and paralysed. My contribution was the LSD and the ecstasy. The LSD would keep his mind busy, hopefully enough to confuse his concentration so I could break into his mind without too much of a struggle. The ecstasy would also help unbalance him, and mellow any internal strife he might otherwise have conjured up. The head rushes he'd experience would also help to throw him off balance. I know they did for me on my first time.

It would take half hour for the drugs to really kick in, so I didn't make any aggressive move just yet. I did take a peek at his mind though, to gauge his defences. I was shocked to see his mind wrapped in shifting coils of multicoloured strands. I saw a kaleidoscope of shimmering colour. Like snakes, the strands twisted through and around each other. This didn't look like the type of shield I practiced against. This man was unconscious and still he created this level of protection for himself. I experienced a small moment of doubt, soon crushed by thoughts of revenge.

When I glanced out of the rear window of the van I saw from the angle of the sun that we were not heading back to the farm. I turned to the Friar and asked him where we were going.

"We're going to the monastery we visited yesterday," he replied. "The monks there can help shield us while you complete your task. It is a revered holy place and official local interference will be minimised. While we have an understanding with the local forces, I don't want to rely on it. Don't worry. We'll be well protected there."

Always with the worry, but in this instance he may be right — I was a little bit concerned. Even with my personal experience of him, I don't think I really accepted Lazarus for the being that the Friar had claimed he was. A man of power no doubt, but I never imagined him as this thing on the floor in front of me, a man shaped miracle that healed himself even while unconscious and drugged. And he wasn't just healing a modest wound, but stitching together a hole that would have killed pretty much anything that walked.

I watched Lazarus closely as the van climbed the bumpy track to the monastery. The drugs appeared to be kicking in. I saw more confusion and less organisation in the squirming mass that protected his mind. That provided me with some small relief at any rate. From the slight twitching in his fingers I guessed that he tried to fight the effects. That was good. That was exactly what I wanted him to be doing.

I looked at the Friar and told him that it was time for another dose. Without comment he injected the contents of another syringe into Lazarus. For anyone else we wouldn't need to do anything else as that would be enough to kill him there and then.

The moment the van stopped outside the monastery, the side door was pulled open. Two of the soldiers jumped out and helped by the waiting monks, carrying Lazarus' body onto a waiting trolley. The rest of us disembarked and followed them into the monastery itself. The body was taken to a small chapel. I felt an uncomfortable tremor as we entered, a chill shiver that travelled down my spine. Probably just all the excitement I thought and dismissed it.

I made myself comfortable on one of the available chairs, and now saw that Lazarus was very high on the drugs we pumped into him. I observed the flowing strands and started to peel away at his defences. It proved much more difficult than I had expected. At first I probed for the imperfections as I had been taught. The constant movement prevented this approach, so I tried teasing at the strands, loosened each one so I could tug it free. As I pulled, it snapped and disappeared. I kept doing this, but the destroyed strands must have regenerated, for I discerned no reduction in the coiling mass.

Next I tried grabbing a clump of the strands to yank them free, but the mass would not move. I tried again with smaller clumps. Eventually I found a weakness and snapped dozens of the wormlike threads. They regenerated themselves as quickly as before. I sighed in frustration and pulled back. For a time I watched the shifting threads. I could discern no pattern, no weakness that I could exploit. They covered the surface of his mind, followed the contours of his skin.

That gave me an idea.

I took a look at the body, turned to the Friar and asked, "Are you sure you don't just want to stake him out in the desert and drop a nuke on him?" I would love to see that. Awesome wouldn't even come close. The Friar didn't go for it, though. He told me to get on with it. I nodded, stood up and approached Lazarus — then with a swift movement jabbed my finger through his eye.

The sudden physical contact struck below the tendrils that defended him and I surged my awareness through this gap. The snakes tried to react to this violent intrusion. Before they were able, I poured more of myself in, quickly enough to block their counterattack. While I pushed from the inside I also ripped away at them from the outside, a two pronged attack that brought success, and with that I was in.

My perspective shifted and I suddenly stood alone, surrounded by the warped landscape of his mind. Above me a maelstrom raged, and below a stormy sea of chaos swirled beneath my feet. Lazarus sensed my invasion and responded. Around me the seas flattened leaving me standing on an ocean of glass. I looked down at the surface and saw there were no ripples as I walked. My reflection formed a ghostly, distorted figure that mocked me for my impertinence. I marched forwards, the direction unimportant, only a metaphor for travelling deeper. Above me the clouds darkened.

When the storm broke it dropped no rain. Only lightning and fire. Lazarus unleashed his fury upon me, using fire and storm to drive me from his psyche. My pain was sudden and immense, a living thing that clutched at me. In its jealousy it promised to never leave me. The lightning lashed at me. I felt my form weakening, convulsed at the touch of the electric barbs.

Tongues of flames rained from the sky, their hunger gnawing at my substance. Searing agony tore across my entire being. I struggled forwards, defying the forces that raged against me. This was a battle of will, his rage against my drive for revenge. I gritted my teeth attempting to continue onwards, but the pain proved too much. I fell; the glassy surface now reflected the storm of fire and darkness.

This wasn't real. I tried to convince myself of the falsity of this ruined reality, but the pain felt all too real. I couldn't deny its existence. The flames chewed upon my flesh — even my bones felt molten. All I felt was Lazarus' wrath unleashed upon me. I met my new mistress of pain, and she clung ever tighter.

It wasn't real.

My suffering belied those words. My skin blackened and blistered, then cracked open and I saw the rawness beneath. Lightning lanced from the sky, struck me over and over again. Whenever I tried to rise, another bolt slammed me down.

Not real.

I couldn't even crawl, the pain too much. Every strike of lightning convulsed me, shredded the burnt flesh with a new wave of agony. My strength faded. I couldn't move any further. This wasn't right — his mind should be broken. How could he defeat me so easily?

Pride gave me the strength to endure, became my guardian angel. I focused my will. I needed to concentrate, to think.

This was his mind, his rules. I couldn't match his strength in his own world, so another approach was needed. I shut myself off from the pain. I forced it to become a background thing. She beckoned me, strangely beguiling, but I must ignore her. This mistress of agony howled her fury at my scorn. I realised that fighting the pain was a battle of attrition I could not win, but the cause of the pain was another matter.

I focused what remained of my will and endured. I channelled my strength to my limbs and staggered to my feet. My ears filled with the demented howls of the storm that engulfed me. I managed a single step. The agony of my seared flesh almost drove me to the floor again.

With a huge effort I managed a second step and I pressed against his rage. It hurt. It hurt so much, but I refused to be beaten, not like this. Not at the first hurdle. I must weather the storm, I must endure. I pictured the delicious revenge against Lazarus.

Suddenly there was some give. I forced another step. A breeze lapped around me, fanning the flames. At first, just for a moment, they bit deeper and in that moment I almost failed. With a scream that drowned out all other sound I surged and managed another step. The will that opposed me shattered, and I stumbled at the sudden release of it. I heard it howl away in the distance.

Triumphantly I stood and let the burnt flesh fall from my bones, watched it disintegrate as it hit the ground. I reshaped my form around my now gleaming skeleton and strode on with a satisfied smile.

The landscape shimmered. There hadn't been a palace before, but now there was. Before me I looked upon an obscene mismatch of opulence: in part a colonial mansion, in others a sultan's palace. I even noticed shapes from European fortresses of the Bavarian style. Huge and loathsome, it exuded wealth and power. The door lay open, welcoming.

The door provided the only way forwards. I had to enter, despite my misgivings.

Inside the mix of styles continued, presented a confusion of luxury. A leery voice bid me welcome as I stepped through the entrance. The massive hall stretched before me. You could land a plane in this room. It was dominated by marble stairs that stretched up to the next floor. Positioned around the walls stood sculpted podiums, each supporting a bust of the rich and famous from throughout history.

"These are nothing compared to what you could be." A fleeting whisper that teased.

At the base of the stairs waited a woman. She looked beautiful and sultry. I didn't recognise her at first, then another shimmer and her face became familiar. Stunned I realised that it was Ms Clarke: a perfected version formed by desire's memory, not by clumsy sight. There she stood, my treasured conquest from all those years ago. She appeared as beautiful and as willing as she ever was. The voice invited me to take her, this lovely creature who once filled me with delights.

I kissed her full lips, savoured the sweet taste of them. My memory of her faded in this moment of seduction, my desire hard at her touch. The kiss extended, swallowed me with its passion. Her skin soft and pliant to the touch. Her garments were flimsy, mere decoration of the perfect beauty beneath.

The moment stretched and I was lost. I surrendered myself to her, to the moment. "This is yours forever," the sibilant voice promised. It should have kept silent. It was an unwelcome intrusion and it denied my power. How dare it! This lovely creature was once mine, through my own strength. I needed no whispered promises to satisfy my urges. I broke free from the embrace, pushed her from me before mounting the stairs.

I paused when I reached the top of the staircase; my feet sank into the deep, lush carpet. Heady scents now tantalized my nose. The voice travelled with me. "Indulge in your desires," it told me. "This house and everything and everyone in it can be yours." I couldn't help but form a mocking smile in response. Of course it could be mine, but it wasn't real. This illusion of material paradise was a trap — a clever one, but a trap nonetheless.

At the top of the stairs another woman waited, a younger form of my mother. She would take care of me, soothe the pain in my soul. More promises from the insidious voice. I kissed her tenderly on the cheek, experiencing a momentary pang of grief as I walked on. This illusion held no power over me.

On this floor the walls were hung with paintings. Delightful works from all of the ages. All around me I saw images famous from hundreds of galleries and museums. Treasures that should be mine, the voice insisted.

This wasn't real. I smiled. But it could be real, the voice asserted.

Onwards I walked, headed deeper into the house. I followed the corridor that wound through impossible angles. I became lost in that maze of decadence. At each turn a new woman awaited, each more lovely than the last. All shades of humanity's beauty represented. All shapes catered for. I was engulfed by this temptation of riches and luxury, my senses bombarded by these seductions of the flesh. I liked this place — if it had been real I would be tempted, but I knew it was a lie. I must seek the end of the maze. Somewhere there would be an exit.

Lazarus would have to do better than this, I thought. I could have owned these delights in the real world. I had no need for the imagined indulgences. The thought bolstered my will. My purpose drove me on.

I heard his rage, distant and all around me. The corridor ahead stretched beyond my sight. I continued walking. I had to maintain momentum. Lazarus cannot hide from me forever.

When the voice finally became silent the exit appeared, a simple wooden door set in the frescoed wall. Without any hesitation I walked through it.

The sudden desolation hammered me.

A featureless grey desert stretched out as far as I could see. It presented an endless sea of despair that I must cross. I heard new voice: the same, but no longer full of promise. Instead it now sounded leaden with sadness. There would be no end, it promised. There would be no help. I would remain forever alone, without even torment for company. I trudged through the grey ash, each step a new weight that slowed me down.

Above me spread a blank grey sky. In the grey desert there were no landmarks. When I turned around I saw that not even my footsteps were visible. There was nothing to catch the eye but the endless horizon that encircled me. I must continue, I thought. The voice said, "Why bother?

What will change? You can never reach the other side of this place. Here is where all hope comes to die."

Each step cut my feet, the fine sand sharp as a razor. Constantly I refreshed the skin, wiped away the wounds, only for them to return when I next placed my foot.

"Your strength cannot help you here. It is sapped by the shroud of despair that covers you." The voice was persuasive, and with its sadness I felt a little of my will drained. "You wanted to die," it said — "just lie down. There will be no pain." I ignored the voice. It was the voice of a trickster, so onwards I walked. To stop would be to die. I must not stop.

That lonely, weak voice continued to whisper, reminding me of the terrible things that had happened. It told me of my failures, of hopes destroyed. In this it erred, for those hopes were not my hopes. I had known sadness, but it didn't kill me then and it wouldn't kill me now. As for misery, I heard it likes company, so let's get on with it.

Again there was that howl of rage. A fury that tore through the sky. It was music to my ears. The desert stretched ever onwards. Finally after what felt like a million steps a shape took form in the desolate haze ahead.

Chapter 40
Death of a miracle

Lazarus waited for me. He stood there in the grey dust, watching me approach. As I walked nearer I saw a tiny stone, almost hidden on the ground behind him. Some instinct told me that this tiny pebble was once a towering mountain. I felt relieved that it no longer was.

"Who are you to deny my vengeance?" Lazarus' voice now sounded stronger than its recent incarnations. Each word was spoken with deliberation and menace. It echoed throughout his mind like the word of God.

"You don't remember me?" I responded.

He looked at me closely, and a moment passed before recognition dawned. "The sacrifice. You have grown stronger." He suddenly seemed more confident. That was his mistake.

"Yes. I vowed we would meet again and I like to keep my word."

"So what now? You do the Friar's bidding?"

"I do my own biding."

"Ah. So this is just revenge."

I gave a little snort. "In part. I also think that stopping the Apocalypse is a worthwhile endeavour."

"Your petty revenge pales in comparison to what was done to me. And nothing is what it seems," he told me and

I noticed his voice had moderated a little. "See what they have taken from me."

With the loss evident in his voice the landscape warped. We were no longer engulfed by the desolate terrain. Now I witnessed Heaven through his eyes and it was glorious. Majestic buildings and structures of such beauty it almost hurt to look at them speared the sky above us. Everywhere I looked there I saw light and radiance. My ears were now awash with harmonies from a choir of millions, each voice singing in concert, complementing each other. Heaven was unity. Every being here worked together as one. There was no self, only the wondrous whole, greater than its constituent parts. Delectable scents overwhelmed my senses, and I felt transported on a current of bliss. I had never witnessed such union, such magnificence. For a moment my heart ached for him and what he had lost.

I could barely imagine the anguish at being torn from such perfection. Even I understood the temptation of being part of a greater whole, to be more than just the self, but it is there that I saw the flaw.

I looked again, not at the Heaven filtered by his memories, but as he truly saw it. It looked the same, felt the same — but it also lacked something. An alien shadow marred the exquisite vision. Heaven formed the domain of all, where everyone combined their will for the greater whole. If you accepted being part of this union then Heaven is what it claimed. But there was no self. There was no individuality, nothing that made each person trapped there unique.

Unity is what helped humanity endure. It was the coming together that made us strong. But it was self, it was always individuals that made us great. Heaven lacked that dimension. It possessed great strength — it owned common purpose — but it did not have everything.

"You see!" Lazarus' broken voice interrupted my thoughts. "You see what they took from me. For one glorious eternal moment I shared myself with Heaven, became one with God. And his son took that from me."

I saw no God there. Unless God was the whole? A mystery to be unravelled, or just another delusion?

"He might have wept while he did it, but the result was the same. I, who was the greatest of his disciples, the most loved, betrayed by the saviour of man."

I tasted his bitterness, but I saw no saviour there either.

"With my Apocalypse all will be swept into Heaven, to be at one with the Almighty. There will be no more pain, no more sorrow, and no more death. Evil and the terrors it creates will be vanquished forever. And it is I that brings salvation to the world, not the son, not the betrayer.

"Join me and together we can be the saviours of the world."

I thought it was nice of him to consider sharing, but he's more than a little confused. The rage that powered him had also warped him. This conversation now bored me. There was nothing for me to learn here. The time had come to end this.

"Your Heaven looks to me no better than the Hell described by the priests of your God. No matter, we end it here. We end it now."

With that rather dramatic statement from me, we clashed. Our wills strained against each other. Our forms battled one another as if still in the physical world. Muscles powered by thought drove blows against each other. I could see that Lazarus was distracted: he wasn't just fighting me, he also fought some inner turmoil that he attempted to hide.

I love it when a plan comes together.

LSD wasn't the drug you wanted to be on if you're fighting. Personally I loved it, but for your first time, a battle to the death was a little harsh.

We continued to battle. He showed no fear, but his defence was weak. He was too distracted and couldn't focus his will. There was no entertainment for me here. After that moment where he held me in thrall with fear I expected more from my revenge. I guess actually planning takes some of the sport from the contest.

My hands became claws as I tore into his form, energetically ripping great chunks from him. I consumed the jelly like lumps. With each mouthful I became filled with his knowledge. With each bite I gained more power. Memories from his past added to my own experiences. With each torn lump I devoured I grew stronger. It tasted foul, but I hungered for more.

The Friar was right: over the past two thousand years this man had become powerful. He had learned knowledge from mystics and men of power from all over the world. And now it was all mine.

It took some time to consume all of Lazarus' being; I ate every scrap until eventually all that remained was his spirit. A bedraggled wisp of a thing, it couldn't touch me, let alone harm me. I stepped towards the pebble on the ground, and with new eyes I saw something within. When I picked up the stone, Lazarus' spirit wailed. It begged for release, to be done with this existence, to return to the communion he once knew.

As I held the stone in my hands, the world was abruptly shattered by the toll of a bell, its ring deafening. It carried within it a voice alien to this mind, but I knew it well: Friar Francis. From light years away I heard his command.

"Destroy the miracle! Destroy it now!"

Ah the poor Friar, he was going to be very angry with me. I twisted the pebble with all my might, crumbling the stone to reveal the secret within. I held the miracle that sustained Lazarus for all this time and now it was mine. It felt light and warm.

That dread bell tolled once more. Again the repeated command.

"For the sake of your immortal soul, destroy the miracle!"

I imagined that the Friar had always been a worrier. Perhaps it was the thought of defiance that encouraged my act. Or maybe it was just a desire for more power. It didn't matter either way. After all I had just destroyed the man who'd terrorised the church for two thousand years and if Lazarus could handle its power I felt sure I could do the same.

I swallowed the miracle and felt its power infuse my whole being. It felt good.

Then it burned.

The landscape around me distorted into a funnel. Its gaping maw opened wide before me. It spun and the spirit of Lazarus was sucked into the maw. He cried now for release, but release of a different sort. He now realised that he had forsaken the path to Heaven. His soul screamed as it fell.

The fire within me raged. The miracle came with a price.

I had stood at this abyss before and gazed into its depths. As before I saw the shapes in the darkness, but the miracle made me immune to its pull. I allowed myself to drift in and as Lazarus' soul was dragged into Hell I took the moment to contemplate what I could see of that infernal place. It was not what I expected.

I struggled against the tempest of fire that flared within me, the sudden influx of power almost too much for my mind to contain. I burned from the inside out and I could not stop it. In the moment before Lazarus' death collapsed his mind I returned to my own mind and opened my eyes.

Chapter 41
Unjust reward

The miracle consumed me.

In my arrogance I assumed I could just take its power for my own. How wrong I was! I battled with this blessed corrosion that seared through my body and soul. I screamed — I couldn't hear it, but I knew that I screamed.

I was still screaming when I returned to my body, my finger still sticky inside Lazarus' cooling eye. I barely saw the shapes of the monks and soldiers around me. I couldn't see clearly, everything appearing as a blur. The Friar's voice was only just audible above my own tormented cries.

"You fool." He sounded almost sad. "You were told to destroy it. This miracle is not for you."

The fire within me was worse than the storm I battled in Lazarus' mind. There was no escape. It scorched every fibre of my being. For the first time in my life I asked for help. I begged the Friar to help me.

"I cannot," he said, not unkindly.

The realisation that I had brought this doom upon myself added a bitter flavour to the pain. The stone floor hard under me as I collapsed, but I hardly felt the impact on my knees. I continued to fight, surging my will against the conflagration that boiled inside me.

I wept tears of fiery anguish. My resistance only inflamed the agony I suffered. My will was not enough to suppress the price for this miracle. Through the flames I could see the abyss. Now the depths taunted me with promised oblivion. For my hubris I will never know that blessed calm. Even the fires of hell would surely be less than this suffering.

The miracle would not let me enter. Once again I must endure and there was no end in sight.

Man shapes loomed over me, strong hands gripped me, lifted me from the floor. The Friar's voice seemed so far away. "I feared this would happen. I knew you would be foolish enough to try this, even as I prayed that you would not."

The sympathy in his voice scalded me. Never had I been so powerful — Lazarus' knowledge and strength were now mine to command. Never had I been so weakened, the miracle all powerful against my efforts.

They carried me from the chapel. The warm sunlight had faded, but the cool air provided me no relief. I was taken to a hidden corner in the monastery. I had little comprehension of what was happening, but I suddenly felt afraid.

"I hoped that you would not take this path, but I prepared in case you did. We cannot help you now." The Friar's voice, soft and distant judged me.

Time passed. I'm left alone with my mistress. She had eagerly returned to seduce me with her torments. Then I realised I was in a tight dark space. With frayed senses I sensed the ancient stone walls closed tight around me.

No, not this. My fear was sharp and immediate.

The surrounding monks said prayers for my soul. Their chants smothered my screams — they prayed for redemption for my release. It was far too late for that.

Suddenly I was pushed back. I thought I was falling, but only for a moment. My failing vision saw the soldiers holding me. The cold metal grasped my limbs. I heard the din of power tools as they bolted me to the wall.

All too late I struggled. It could not end like this. My efforts were weak, pitiful. My own power was both great and feeble. The Friar urged me to restrain myself, that it would be better this way. Solid metal now bound me to the wall behind. More activity and the walls closed in further.

They fixed a mask to my face, muffling my voice. I tried to cast my mind out, to launch my awareness to safety, but the combined chants of the monks smothered my effort. Enclosing me with their own power they neutralised my abilities. Their presence faded from my awareness as the wall was sealed, brick by brick. I could not see it, but I knew it was happening.

When the final brick was placed, it left only me, alone in the darkness. No, not quite alone — I had my new terrible mistress for company.

Continued in 'Conversations in the Abyss'

Thanks for reading, if you enjoyed this book then please leave a review where you bought it from – reviews are an indie author's life blood and are always appreciated!

You can discover my other books on my blog:

http://thecultofme.blogspot.co.uk/

Printed in Great Britain
by Amazon